Magic in Mount Holly

Also By Nicole A Mullaney

Ivy & Mistletoe
The Maltese Holiday
Deck the Heart

Also Check out Books by Character, Ethan Dulane
Ethan Dulane is a Character Created by
Candy Cain & Nicole Mullaney for Joy & Hope

Joy & Hope

Watch the Books You've Read
Movies by Writer/Director Candy Cain

Ivy & Mistletoe
The Maltese Holiday
Deck the Heart
Joy & Hope
Magic in Mount Holly

For Romance Reads with Mature Content
Check out Books by Nikki A Lamers

The Unforgettable Summer
Unforgettable Nights
Unforgettable Dreams
Unforgettable Memories
The Unforgettable One
Unforgettable Mistakes

Dreams Lost and Found
Finding Home

By Nicole A Mullaney

Based on the Screenplay by Candy Cain

Table of Contents

Copyright

Cover design by Heartly Creations

Cover photo by Benjamin Bryant

Dedication

For Juliette Marotta,
Who shares her own magic,
As a mom, grandmother, friend and artist.

Prologue

'Twas Two Weeks before Christmas, in a sleepy ski town,
but no one was smiling, everyone was quite down.

The restaurants were empty, the chairlifts were still,
the weather was warm, not even a chill.

Yes, it felt more like May and not like December,
and they needed the snow to bring the tourists, remember?

The people were sad, Santa was melancholy,
in this small, remote hamlet, by the name of Mount Holly.

No one was spending, many stalls had to close,
but one woman went out on a limb, I suppose.

Her family behind her, best friend by her side,
a magical gift from St. Nick as her guide.

Her stomach in knots, she was under such stress,
not knowing if she'd fail or become a success.

Her name was Noelle and she really loved art,
so, she opened a gallery as big as her heart.

Chapter 1

Noelle

I pull my sleek, long, blonde hair back into a ponytail, and twist a tan rubber band around it, tucking it into a messy bun to keep it out of my way. I take a deep breath as I push up the sleeves of my pale, aqua blue, crew neck, thin, oversized sweater and tack up another gold tinsel streamer for decoration along another display table in my new shop, an art gallery with artwork I dream up and create.

Then, I turn back towards all my paintings leaning against the long, white wall, looking closely at those remaining. I take my time assessing each one. I purse my lips in thought as I attempt to decide which ones I still want to display. I need to make sure I showcase a variety of my artwork tonight to give people a good idea of what I'm able to do. I'll have to find a spot for the rest of them in the back room, until I do have the space to exhibit each one up front, but I have no idea when that might be. Hopefully tonight goes really well and I won't have a huge stack of my projects left in the back room collecting dust.

I look up and down the long narrow room stretching towards the large storefront picture windows, the bottom of the sill only a foot from the ground. I'm almost immediately blinded by a huge vacant space near the middle of the wall, right in the center of a row of my landscape oil paintings. I reach for another one of my completed canvases I believe will fit in there. Carefully picking it up, I gently hang it on the wall between two of my other creations. Then, I stand back taking in the whole view. I want to make sure I place it in the right location on the wall to complement the work around it. I believe little things like that can make all the difference in how an individual views the piece of art. My new painting is on a smaller canvas, a scene of the Italian countryside with rolling hills and blue skies covering it. I narrow my eyes and pinch my lips together in thought. It seems to fit, but I really want everything to be perfect.

"It looks good," my best friend, Daphne, encourages me. I glance in her direction before taking one last look at the arrangement of the paintings on the wall. I've always admired her quirky sense of style. Like me, she's wearing cropped denim jeans, cuffed at the bottom, but she has hers paired with a soft gray tight-knit sweater dress hanging just above her knees and adorable short, black suede boots, while my navy "Duck" boots are more for working with my artwork or walking outside in the snow or rain. She's slightly taller than my five-feet, seven-inches in height with natural lightly bronzed skin, silky, long, straight, black hair, big, dark, coffee brown eyes, rounded face with high cheekbones and a light spattering of freckles over the bridge of her nose. I'm the opposite of her, physically, with my straight, long, light blonde hair, fair ivory skin, oval face with high cheekbones and pale blue-gray eyes. I'm incredibly grateful to have her in my life. She's always there for me no matter what's going on in either of our lives, while I do everything I can to do the same for her. I really couldn't ask for a better best friend and I would never want to.

I bite my lip and release it as I spin back towards her, forcing a smile. She's standing near the new silver and black cash register as she gathers holiday colored helium filled balloons in her hands; one red, one green and one white, all with colorful ribbons hanging down from them to keep them grounded. I pause, watching as she loosely ties them together before she hands them to me and then begins repeating the process. I heave a sigh and stride over to a five-foot, white table, in the middle of my new art studio

10

and tie them onto one of the narrow, silver legs underneath, hoping to keep them in place.

"My new art studio," I repeat to myself under my breath, still slightly in shock about my reality. I can't believe I'm actually opening up my own shop at the age of twenty-five. It's almost harder to believe it's in the same small, New England town I grew up in. I've always loved Mount Holly, with its quaint Main Street, including a gas station on the opposite end as me, a bank, a hair salon, a local market, a bakery, a florist, a variety store, some local gift shops and restaurants, such as Rooster's Café and Cuppa' Joe, as well as some local offices. My new storefront, "The First Noelle," will be opening right around the corner from Daphne's Doggie Palace, my best friend's pet grooming business. Plus, I'm right next door to the coffee shop. For me, that's a good thing. I really enjoy my coffee breaks when I'm working on my artwork. Time does tend to slip away from me now and then when I immerse myself in one of my projects. Besides, the owner, Joe and his wife, Vivienne are incredibly kind people. I know they'll be wonderful business neighbors, just like they have always been fantastic friends to my whole family.

I turn back to Daphne and begin rearranging some of the earrings, necklaces and other jewelry set up at the counter to better showcase the designs. She ties the ribbons of the last balloon bouquet and loosely ties them near the register. Glancing up at them, she smiles in satisfaction and looks over at me proudly announcing, "I think that should do it."

I turn slowly in a circle, letting my eyes skim all around the room and at the arrangements on the walls, all decorated with a bunch of my paintings, plus a few local artists added in for both variety of tastes and support. I've scattered some of my other creations, such as my jewelry, my bags, clay vases, small sculptures and other types of artwork, throughout the room on shelves, hooks, small display cabinets, or on one of the long thin tables we set up for that purpose. Satisfied with the results, I turn and stride towards Daphne as she walks around the front counter, meeting me halfway. I wrap my arms around her, squeezing her tightly as she happily returns my hug. "Daphne, thank you!" I murmur, gratefully.

She releases me and gives me a look of disbelief. "Oh, come on," she smirks. "You don't need to thank me." Arching her eyebrows in challenge, she reminds me, "You're my best friend. Do you really think I'd make you decorate for your grand opening all by yourself?"

A slow smile spreads across my face and I squeal with excitement. "Grand opening!" I repeat. "Oh, I'm so excited!" I feel the thunderous pounding of my heart and I place my hand flat on my chest hoping to help calm my nerves.

"You should be," Daphne encourages me. "You put your heart and soul into this place, Noelle," she declares with the kind of pride only someone who loves you can portray effortlessly warming my heart.

"I couldn't have done it without you," I tell her, sincerely.

She chuckles and waves me off, insisting, "You can say that after tonight's opening is a big success."

She always knows exactly what to say. "Trust me, I will," I declare. I bite my lower lip, in hesitation and look away, beginning to fiddle anxiously with the decorations already hung neatly along the counter, without really doing anything at all. "Do you really think it's going to be a success?" I question anxiously, without sparing a glance in her direction.

Out of the corner of my eye, I see her nodding her head in affirmation as she responds without delay. "Yeah, of course!" she exclaims. "Why wouldn't it be?"

I grimace, suddenly feeling slightly unsure. I'm proud of my work, but you never know what people will like when it comes to art, just like with reading a book or watching a movie. Everyone has his or her own taste and their tastes might not include my work. Ironically, that's also one of the reasons I love art so much, almost anything can be beautiful to someone's eye, depending on their perspective. Besides, I know I'd always regret it if I never tried. "I don't know…" I finally mumble, releasing a heavy sigh.

Her eyebrows draw down in concern. "What's wrong with you, Girl?" she gently prompts.

I sigh again, with my shoulders sagging, ready to voice to Daphne what I continue to ask myself. I attempt to gulp down the lump in my throat as I begin moving red and white candy canes around in a clear glass trifle bowl, as if they're art and not treats for my customers tonight. Taking a deep breath, I blurt out the question gnawing at the back of my mind, continuing to avoid her worried gaze, "What if I'm not good enough? What if people don't like my work?"

Her eyes widen in surprise. "Are you serious?" she prods, not expecting me to respond. She steps towards me, gently placing her hand on my forearm in support. "Noelle, you're one of the most incredible artists I've ever seen," she emphasizes, "and I've been to the Louvre," she reminds me, grinning wide.

I roll my eyes at her comment. I'm sure she's exaggerating. "I'm being serious, Daph," I state, pleading with her, my anxiety rising.

"So am I!" she claims, vehemently. She steps up behind me, softly nudging my arm, urging me to turn towards her. I cautiously turn and meet her gaze. "Noelle, you were at the top of your class at the Art Conservatory. You went there on a full ride, for Heaven's sake. You're good, Noelle," she emphasizes. Grasping both my hands in hers, she reiterates, "You're better than good. You're great." Looking back at her, I try to see the truth in her eyes, but they show nothing but pride, love and complete sincerity.

My chest tightens, as I'm nearly overwhelmed with my feelings of love for her. I'm thankful to have such an amazing friend who has so much faith and trust in me. I offer her a half-smile, truly grateful for all her efforts. "Thanks, Daph," I murmur, appreciatively. "Sometimes I just feel like," I pause, pinching my lips together, attempting to come up with the words to describe the uncertainty I'm feeling. "I don't know..." I grumble. I shrug my shoulders, finishing on a harsh exhale and trail off with a wince in frustration.

"Like you're going to fail?" she prompts.

I nod my head sadly and quietly confirm, "Yeah."

"Welcome to the wonderful world of small businesses, my friend," she proclaims sarcastically. She laughs, the light sound giving me some of the comfort I'm seeking. "It feels like you're about to jump from a plane and you don't know if your parachute is going to work, right?" she inquires, with an arch of her eyebrow.

My eyes widen in surprise, somehow still amazed at how she can practically read my thoughts. Then again, that's one of the reasons she's been my best friend for so long. She knows me better than anyone, just like I do her. I exhale slowly and nod my head in agreement, a small smile playing on my lips. "Oh, my goodness, exactly," I concur.

Daphne pushes her shoulders back as if she's about to deliver a speech. She looks into my eyes, and nods her head in acknowledgement, enlightening me, "I know. I feel it, too, sometimes."

My eyes widen, slightly shocked to hear her admission. She always seems so put together and on top of everything with her pet grooming business as well as everything else going on in her life at the time. "What gets you through it?" I prod.

I notice another hint of a smile and her eyes sparkling. Then, she claims, "Knowing that my best friend will be holding a giant net for me if I fail."

I give her a grateful smile. "Thanks, Daph," I murmur.

She pulls me in close and gives me another encouraging hug, while my arms wrap reflexively around her. "You're going to be great," she insists, mumbling into my ear.

Smiling, I claim, "You always say that."

Then, she steps back, releasing me and my arms drop to my sides. "Because it's true," she insists. She lifts her hand, glancing at a small silver watch on her wrist, checking for the time. Her eyes widen and she jumps slightly. "Oh! I gotta' run. Mrs. McCoy is bringing Precious in for a cut and manicure," she informs me.

I cross my arms over my chest and arch my eyebrows in astonishment. "You're giving a poodle a manicure?" I question, disbelief clear in my tone.

She smirks and rolls her eyes. "A french manicure," she clarifies, giggling softly. "Don't even get me started," she mumbles, shaking her head and grinning in amusement. "I'll see you at dinner, tonight," she proclaims. She waves as she spins on her heel, turning towards the front door. "Bye!" she calls over her shoulder, without looking back.

"Bye, Daph," I reply.

I watch her walk outside before I take one more look around my shop, taking it all in, feeling overcome with emotion. Taking a deep breath, I slowly breathe out, trying to get both my body and my mind to relax. I smile to myself and turn towards the small room at the back of the store on the left that I'm attempting to turn into my art studio. It's still a mess, but I guess it will just take some time to get everything put away and set up the way I want it. I'm trying to find a place for everything, so I don't have to store all my things at my parents' house anymore giving me easier access and giving them their space back. I have gray, plastic shelves filled with a lot of my art supplies, including paints, paintbrushes, jewelry wire, beads of various colors, shapes and sizes, a potter's wheel, clay, various types, styles and designs of paper, sketch pads, blank canvases, completed canvases, as well as a small rectangular wooden table and a tall, 3-legged black metal easel to use to create my paintings.

I set up plates, cups and cookies on a small table to bring out later tonight before I set up my easel. Then, I pick up a medium-sized blank white canvas and place it on the easel sideways as I try to decide what I want to paint. I feel like working on something will help keep my mind off tonight, so I stop second guessing everything I've already done. I'm so nervous. Daphne's words of encouragement help, but...I take a deep breath and gulp down the lump in my throat again. It's beginning to feel permanent. Maybe getting lost in a painting for a little while is exactly what I need. I pick up a paintbrush and begin mixing paints on a clean palette. I tap the hard end of the paintbrush against my chin as I stare at the blank canvas, attempting to come up with something simple, yet fun, but my mind keeps coming up blank like the canvas in front of me.

Suddenly, the entrance bell rings, interrupting my thoughts. "I forgot to lock the front door," I mumble softly to myself. I freeze and listen for more movement.

"Hello? Anyone here?" a man's voice calls out.

I set my palette and paintbrush down and rush out to the front of the shop. I find an older gentleman standing tall in front of a set of shelves perusing some of my artwork. He has short hair so gray it's nearly as white as the snow with a matching mustache and beard, neatly trimmed. He's dressed casually in dark blue jeans, a red, white and black plaid, flannel shirt and a dark green winter coat, adorned with a wool collar. "Hi!" I greet him cheerfully. He turns to face me, his bright, blue eyes sparkling, his cheeks rosy from the cool air outside and his smile very friendly. I can't help but smile back at him, a feeling of familiarity rushing through me. "I'm so sorry," I apologize, "but the shop is closed," I inform him.

"But your door was open," he replies, politely.

I nod in agreement. "I know, I'm sorry. I forgot to lock it after my friend left," I concede, regrettably.

He glances downwards, appearing immensely sad, making my heart tighten for him. It gives me the urge to want to do something to make it better. "I see," he mumbles appearing almost heartbroken, but that doesn't make any sense.

"You are more than welcome to come back tonight for the grand opening," I encourage him. The last thing I want to do is to turn new customers away. "We'll have hot chocolate and gingerbread," I add, hoping to entice him to return later.

He smiles brightly and pats his round belly in response. "I do love my gingerbread," he happily admits. He chuckles, the sound low, deep and joyful, growing louder. "Ho, Ho, Ho!" His melodic laughter feels contagious and I begin to giggle along with him.

"It starts at seven," I advise.

He grimaces and offers me an apologetic smile. "I'm afraid I can't make it. The missus is home sick, and I need to look after her. I was just passing through on my way home," he explains, his eyes and face full of regret.

"I'm so sorry to hear that," I reveal. He seems like such a kind man. "I'll tell you what," I begin, "You take a look around and I'll grab you some gingerbread cookies to take home with you."

He smiles wide, his whole face lighting up at my offer. "Deal," he announces, happily, accepting my proposal.

He turns back towards the shelves and continues to gaze at my artwork, filling me with nervous energy and excitement. I'm thrilled to have someone here, but I'm also anxious to find out what people will think of my work. I can't help but wonder if this will be what I'm going to feel like all night.

I spin around and stride back towards my art studio. I lift the lid off a large, round tray filled with gingerbread cookies, sugar cookies, and chocolate cookies. Setting it to the side, I grab a few of the gingerbread cookies for the gentleman and an extra one for his wife, as well. Maybe it will help her feel better. It can't hurt. I put them inside a small container and gently place the container in a white, paper gift bag. I loop a red ribbon through the handles of the bag and tie it in a pretty bow, hoping it helps make it appear more festive. I replace the lid, hoping to keep the cookies fresh for tonight. Then, I turn and stride back towards the front of the shop grasping the handles of the bag in my right hand.

I lift my head as I pass by the cash register, finding my shop empty. "Hello?" I call out, puzzled, although, there's nowhere he could be hiding in this open space. My eyebrows draw down in confusion as I saunter towards the front door. I push the door open and step outside, halting just underneath my pine store sign hanging overhead, attached to the building with a black wrought iron arm and

The First Noelle painted on it in black on both sides. I stand on the sidewalk, looking in both directions as if at a crosswalk, but the sidewalk remains empty. "Huh," I mumble in bewilderment.

I turn around and stride all the way through my store, continuing towards the back door, just in case. I push the heavy door open and take a step outside into the wide alley, but again find no one around. I hear the sound of a door closing with a bang coming from behind me, causing me to startle and spin around. A tall, thin, man with wavy brown hair, appearing to be about the same age as me, exits through the door of Cuppa' Joe. He's carrying a large black garbage bag in one hand as he strides towards the large green dumpster.

As he comes closer, I instantly notice his extreme good looks making my heart skip a beat. He's wearing dark blue jeans, a dark green, waffled thermal with a black button at his neck, a red, white and gray flannel shirt over the top, but left unbuttoned and hanging loose along with black sneakers. His broad shoulders and lean, hard form make it obvious he's extremely fit. Attempting to push my roaming thoughts aside, I swiftly step up to him before he turns away from the dumpster. I bite my lower lip, holding back my gasp with him so close. He has deep green eyes, a chiseled jaw and a small, adorable dimple on his chin. I quietly clear my throat and prompt, "Excuse me. Did you see a man leave my shop?"

He lifts his gaze to mine and smiles at me, enhancing his good looks even more and nearly taking my breath away. I pause, slightly taken aback and wondering who he is.

Chapter 2

Tyler

I wipe down the counter near the coffee machines and then toss the rag in the sink, before I look up, grinning at Mandy, humming along to the Christmas song playing on the radio. She's been working for my uncle at Cuppa' Joe for about three years now, to help her pay for college. She's a sweet girl and a very hard worker. She has her straight, long, blonde hair tied up in a high ponytail to keep it out of her face while she's working. She's dressed in our typical uniform for baristas; black pants, a black polo shirt, with a logo on the left side of her chest and a red and white striped apron over her head and tied around her back. "Christmas," she sings the last line of the song playing softly over the speakers, blushing as she suddenly remembers she has an audience. Pretending I didn't hear her, I reach down, pulling out clean pint glasses used for iced drinks if the customer plans to stay here to eat or drink and setting them on top of the bar.

A bell rings above the door alerting us to a customer entering the coffee shop, his feet tapping on the wood floors as he approaches the counter. Mandy lifts her blue-eyed gaze up to greet him with a broad smile. "Hi, welcome to Cuppa' Joe. May I help you?" she inquires, professionally.

The man has thick black hair, gray eyes and appears to be about the same height and build as me, but the same age as Mandy. It's not that I'm old at twenty-eight, but I'm not in college anymore either. He's dressed casually in faded blue jeans and a dark blue sweatshirt as he greets her with a warm familiarity. "Hi, Mandy," he grins. "I'm going to take a minute to look at the menu first," he advises her.

"Okay," she smiles and nods her head in acknowledgement. "Take your time," she prods as she begins cleaning off the counter in front of her while she waits patiently for his order.

This might be a good time to step away for a minute. "Mandy, I'm going to head out back to take the garbage out. I'll be right back," I inform her.

She looks up at me and acknowledges, "Okay."

I make my way around the counter, into the small seating area and open the enclosed container holding the garbage can. I slide the black bin out and pull out the bag. I quickly tie it off and momentarily set it at my feet, while I replace the bin with a new bag, before I slide it back in and close it up. I pick up the garbage bag and stride right for the back door, barely noticing the festive Christmas decorations as I walk past.

It hasn't felt much like Christmas with Uncle Joe so sick, but now that he's doing better, maybe I'll be able to get more into the holiday spirit. I think if it would finally snow, that would definitely help get everyone in town in more of a Christmas spirit. I heave a sigh, tired from working a long day on my feet. This job is incredibly different from what I'd been doing only last week, but I know I'm exactly where I'm supposed to be. Ironically, I'm already enjoying working here so much more than I did my old job; a job I worked very hard to get. I guess that's the universe telling me I've made the right decision, for more than one reason, although I never once second-guessed my choice.

I push the back door open and step into the small alley behind Cuppa' Joe, the door swinging shut behind me with a bang. The broken blacktop and gravel are all that's found between my closest neighbors' stores and mine. I walk straight for the large green garbage bin, quickly lifting the black lid and dropping the bag inside, before I let the lid fall back in place. I dust off my hands on my jeans and turn back towards the coffee shop with my head down.

A woman steps in front of me to get my attention, stopping me in my tracks and taking me by surprise; I usually don't run into anyone back here. I lift my gaze, finding a tall, thin, beautiful woman standing in front of me. She seems to be about four or five inches shorter than me. She has platinum blonde hair piled high on top of her head and big, pale, blue eyes, highlighted by her long eyelashes. Her high cheekbones appear slightly pink from the cool air, a similar tone to her light rose-colored, heart-shaped lips.

She questions, "Excuse me. Did you see a man out here?" She pauses and then adds, "He was just leaving my shop?"

Her eyebrows are drawn down seeming puzzled as she looks around before bringing her blue eyes back to me as she points behind her to the back door of the new shop. I take a deep breath to get my bearings, realizing she must be the new shop owner and Cuppa' Joe's new neighbor. "A man?" I reiterate. I glance all around me, attempting to figure out who she might be looking for, but there's absolutely no one in sight.

She nods in confirmation, "Yes. White hair, white beard, kind of chubby," she describes, trailing off.

I can't help but smirk at her depiction. She has to be kidding. I sarcastically reply, "Answers to the name of Kris Kringle?" I chuckle softly at my own joke.

"Excuse me?" she prompts. Her eyebrows draw down even further, obviously perplexed by my remark.

I instantly stop laughing and clear my throat, hoping she's not offended. "Oh, I'm sorry," I apologize. "I thought you were kidding," I attempt to explain. I shake my head and try again, telling her, "No, I haven't seen anyone come out of your shop, except Daphne and she went out the front."

"What about the back?" she repeats.

I shake my head again and confirm, "Nope, just me."

She opens her mouth to say something else, but she suddenly stops, snapping her mouth closed. Her eyes widen and she arches her eyebrows as her face suddenly softens. "You know Daphne?" she questions, registering my comment.

I shrug and reply, "Yeah. She came by yesterday and introduced herself. I'm Tyler," I murmur, introducing myself. I grin and hold out my hand for her to shake. She smiles, causing my heart to skip a beat as she places her small, soft, warm hand in mine. "I'm the new manager at Cuppa' Joe," I enlighten her.

"Noelle," she replies, introducing herself.

She releases my hand and I reluctantly let go, instantly feeling the loss and giving me the urge to reach back out for her. Needing to do something with my hands, I motion to the shop behind us, finally understanding the name. "The First Noelle," I repeat the name of her store, aloud. "I get it. It's cute," I compliment, flashing another grin.

She returns my smile, her cheeks turning a little pink from my praise, warming me from the inside. "Thanks," she responds. "It was my mom's idea," she admits sheepishly. She pauses and tilts her head slightly to the side as she looks back at me. "Are you and Joe coming to the grand opening tonight?" she prompts.

I attempt to contain my reaction, barely able to hold back my flinch at the casual mention of my uncle. It's been a rough week in our family, although it's finally getting better. "Oh. I guess you didn't hear what happened to Joe," I mumble, trailing off. My chest tightens and my stomach twists every time I even think about it. I feel terrible for my uncle and my aunt for that matter. I'm just grateful he

23

seems to be doing better and that I'm here to help them out now.

Noelle's eyes widen in both surprise and concern. "Something happened to Joe?" she blurts out, anxiously.

I grimace and release a heavy sigh. "Yeah," I admit, with a stiff nod. "He just got home from the hospital today," I inform her.

Her mouth drops slightly open, as her hand flies up to cover it in shock. "Oh, no!" she exclaims. "What happened?" she prods.

"He had a little episode with his heart," I concede, regretfully. "Doctors said that he needs to take it easy, you know, with all of the stress with the business," I apprise her, gesturing to the coffee shop behind me.

"That's terrible!" she expresses, sincerely. "I had no idea that Cuppa' Joe was so stressful," she claims, her eyebrows drawn together in concern.

I shake my head and elaborate, "It's not the business. It's the lack of business." I heave another sigh and give her a small shrug, before I attempt to end the conversation about my uncle. It's obvious she cares for him, so I do want her to know. It's just still hard for me to talk about, since everything happened so recently. "But I'm sure you know what I mean," I grumble, attempting to wave it off.

She shakes her head in denial. "Actually, I don't," she declares. "I haven't even started yet," she reminds me. "It's that bad?" she questions, her eyebrows suddenly creased with worry.

I force a smile in attempt to give her some encouragement. "Maybe it will be different for you," I convey. I hope my simple words will give her even a little bit of comfort. It has to be tough enough opening up your own business. She doesn't need me worrying her further. I take a deep breath and try to elaborate on our current business situation in this town for those of us that depend on the foot traffic. "He just really counts on the ski crowd this time of year. It's when he does the most business," I claim. "And since it hasn't even snowed yet," I add, trailing off. I'm sure she comprehends my insinuation without elaborating further.

"There hasn't been any business," she finishes my statement. I nod my head slowly in confirmation and give her a sad smile. "I see," she mumbles. "I'm so sorry," she murmurs, her eyes filled with empathy. "Can I do anything to help?" she offers.

My chest tightens, appreciating the offer, but I shake my head in response. "No, but thanks. I'll tell him you asked about him," I apprise her. "I'm running the coffee shop until he gets better," I reiterate.

"Won't that be a while?" she prompts.

I nod my head in confirmation and give a shrug of my shoulders, as if it doesn't matter. Then again, to me, it doesn't matter how long I'm here. In fact, I might never leave. I'll do anything for them, just like they have always done for me. "Sure, but I'm his nephew. I gotta' take care of my family," I announce, nonchalant.

She nods her head in understanding. Then, she gives me a half-hearted smile, causing my own heart to clench briefly, before loosening enough to speak. "That's really nice of you," she recognizes.

I feel my face heat in response. I rub the back of my neck uncomfortably and shrug like it's no big deal. Then, I take a deep breath and drop my hand back to my side. "Uncle Joe and Aunt Vivienne helped put me through college. It's the least I can do to help them," I proclaim, unexpectedly admitting more to her than even I had planned, but it's true. I couldn't imagine being anywhere

25

else, but here, while he gets better and maybe even long after that, as well. Family always comes first, and Uncle Joe and Aunt Viv are my family.

She nods her head in both acknowledgement and admiration, causing my cheeks to turn a deeper shade of red. Then with sincerity shining in her eyes, she insists, "If you need anything, please, just let me know."

I grin back at her in appreciation. "Thanks," I reply simply. I gulp down the sudden lump in my throat and continue, as I attempt to hold back the look of hope I feel growing in my gut. I hold her gaze and enlighten her, "I just moved here yesterday. I might take you up on that."

Another slight blush fills her cheeks, broadening my grin. She shifts on her feet and swiftly changes the subject. "Well, I hope you come tonight," she emphasizes, looking up at me from underneath her long lashes.

"Is that an invitation?" I prod, playfully.

She nods in confirmation, "Yes. Seven PM. Daphne will be here, too. We can introduce you to some people," she suggests, trying to entice me further to make it tonight. Although, I don't think her invitation needs any kind of enhancement. I would want to come to her opening tonight just to have the chance to get to know her better anyway, but I'm not about to admit that to her when we just met. I don't want to scare her away by being too forward when she obviously already has a lot going on.

"Great," I state, grinning. "I'll be there," I announce.

She hands me the white gift bag she's been clasping this whole time. The handles are tied together simply, with a shiny, red, curled ribbon. "Here," she offers. I reach out and take the bag from her. My fingers gently brush over hers as I grasp it, sending a tingling sensation up my arm. "Please give this to Joe for me," she requests.

26

"What is it?" I question, curiously. I peek between the handles, attempting to see the bag's contents.

"Gingerbread cookies," she enlightens me. I inhale deeply, suddenly able to smell the sweet scent of gingerbread and cinnamon. My mouth starts to water and my tongue slips out to lick my lips in response. "Don't you eat them," she smirks, playfully warning me. "There will be plenty at my grand opening. Hot chocolate, too," she adds.

"Yes, Ma'am," I agree, the corners of my mouth twitching up in amusement. "Well," I hesitate, trying to come up with a reason not to say goodbye to her right now. With nothing instantly coming to mind, I relent, finally telling her, "I'll see you tonight."

She nods in agreement and rocks slightly back on her heels, before taking a step back. "Bye, Tyler," she murmurs, sweetly.

My smile widens as I hold her gaze for a brief moment. "See you later, Noelle," I reply. She returns my smile, causing my heart to skip a beat. Then, she spins on her heel and strides back towards her shop, without looking back. I watch her, until she completely disappears, as the back door of The First Noelle closes behind her with a loud click.

"Noelle," I mumble her name under my breath, a smile playing on my lips. I chuckle softly to myself, grateful to finally feel a little bit lighter after such a tough week. First hearing about Uncle Joe, then making it an instant decision to move immediately. I worked fast, but it still took time tying up everything there, including leaving my job, packing up enough at my apartment to get by, knowing I'd have to return to completely empty it out, and trying to make it here as quickly as possible, wanting to see him with my own eyes to make sure he's okay, before finally starting at Cuppa' Joe to help out and still trying to help at the house as much as possible.

I turn and stride back across the alley and in through the back door of Cuppa' Joe. I want to take care of a few things before I leave and now, I'd really like to get out of here on time, if not early. I suddenly have somewhere I want to be tonight, and I don't want to miss it. Plus, I still want to go home to my aunt and uncle's house to help out, as well as shower and change after working all day. I step up to the sink and immediately wash my hands. Then, I begin rinsing the dirty dishes and loading them into the dishwasher, while Mandy finishes up with a customer up front. I smile to myself and allow my mind to wander while I work. My gorgeous new business neighbor, Noelle, is the first thing that crosses my mind. I'm excited to get to know her. Hopefully we'll both have the time and it's something she wants as well. I guess I'll find out.

Chapter 3

Noelle

I step back into my shop and lock the door behind me. Then, I stride towards the front door and do the same, clicking the lock into place. I don't want anyone else to walk inside before the opening tonight. I need to be ready next time someone steps through the front door. I turn away from the door and make my way towards my art studio in the back. Just before I get to the threshold, I suddenly stop as I catch a glimpse of something out of the corner of my eye. My eyes narrow at the bright, cherry red bow on the counter near my cash register. "That wasn't there before," I mumble to myself, as my eyebrows draw down in confusion.

I swiftly change direction and slowly approach the counter, instead. A smile slowly spreads across my face the moment I realize what the bow is attached to. A brand-new paintbrush rests on the counter, with a small square card taped to it. I pause, looking around to see if the person who left it, might still be inside, even though there's not really anywhere to hide. "Hello?" I call out, but no one answers.

I spin back towards the counter and pick up the white card, decorated with a glittery silver snowflake on the front, excited to find out who it's from. I flip it open and read the simple message inside aloud, *"To Noelle, Love Santa."*

I smile to myself, amused. Daphne must have left this here for me to find. I happily murmur out loud, "Thanks, Santa."

I claim the paintbrush, thrilled to get this thoughtful gift. I saunter back into my art studio, admiring the paintbrush. I slide the bow off the paintbrush and set it on the shelf next to me, anxious to try it out. I love testing new brushes to help me figure out what kinds of paintings I prefer to use it for. I like different brushes for different types of painting, but I find every artist I know sees it a little differently, but what fun would art be if we all did things the same way?

I slip a red apron on over my head and tie it behind my back, hoping to give my clothes a little bit of protection. I stand in front of the blank canvas with the new paintbrush in my hand. I get a tingling sensation deep in my gut and I'm suddenly inspired. I know exactly what I want to paint. I reach for my paints, one tube at a time, adding a few shades of brown, yellow, black and white paint to my palette. I pause to look at the blank canvas, attempting to decide where I want to begin, as the familiar smell of paint fills the room. I dip the paintbrush into one of the lighter brown paints and lightly brush the canvas in short, even strokes, allowing my hand to take over the brush like an extension of my arm, expressing my vision, my thoughts and my feelings. I almost immediately get lost in my movements and creating something from nothing. The motions of taking the brush to my palette, across the canvas and back feel methodic and calming as I attempt to transfer the image in my head to the surface in front of me.

Sometimes when I'm painting, it feels as if my hand and the paintbrush take over without my consent, but I almost always find the result to be exactly what I believe I'm trying to convey. Over the years, I've found that painting has been my favorite medium to express and control my emotions. It has continuously been a way to help me think when I have something on my mind, calm me down when I'm anxious, or even feel more like myself when I'm feeling lost. It also helps me share my happiness or love of something or someone. I adore all kinds of art and creativity, but painting is without a doubt my passion. I love how it helps keep me grounded and focused, even if that focus is on the painting itself. Now, with the grand opening of The First Noelle finally happening tonight, I need my art to do all those things and so much more. Hopefully, people will like my work and it will elicit whatever feelings they're searching for in them, drawing them to my work. Although, I can't stop my fear of failure, I desperately want my new shop to become a success, so I'll be able to share my passion with the world. I take a deep breath and exhale slowly. "Tonight's opening just has to go well," I mumble to myself, feeling hopeful.

Tyler

I grab another handful of coffee stirrers, filling the silver container for the customers, before I make my way back around behind the counter. I step up next to Mandy, knowing she's closing tonight as she refills one of the coffee canisters with fresh coffee grounds. "Do you need anything before I go?" I inquire.

She shakes her head in response, while she finishes what she's doing. Then, she glances at me and reaffirms, "No, thanks, Tyler. I've got it."

I nod my head in acknowledgment and murmur my gratitude, "Thanks." I turn and walk to the back of the shop, stepping into the office, passing over the desk with papers stacked neatly in organized piles. I grab my black quilted winter coat off the hook on the back wall, and slip it on, striding towards the front of the café.

A woman, bundled up in a pale pink winter coat and hat, walks towards the entrance. I push the door open and hold it for her with a broad, welcoming smile. She slips inside, walking past me as she murmurs her appreciation, "Thank you."

I nod in acknowledgement and glance towards Mandy standing behind the counter. "I'll see you tomorrow, Mandy," I call.

She waves as I let the door swing shut behind the customer. I make my way to the gravel parking lot and my white sedan. I slide in behind the wheel and make the short drive to my aunt and uncle's house, noticing the addition of more Christmas decorations along the quaint Main Street since my arrival yesterday. There's now thick green garland accented with pine cones and berries, entwined with white lights and wrapped around the old fashioned light posts all through town. Attached at the top of each pole is a large green wreath, accessorized with round, silver and gold ornaments, as well as a large red bow. More stores have joined in, enhancing their storefront decorations and windows as well, but it still doesn't feel quite like Christmas, not yet anyway.

I pull into the driveway at Aunt Vivienne and Uncle Joe's house and park, hopping out of the car. I shut the door behind me and glance up at the minimal decorations on the modest colonial style home. We have a simple light shining on the red front door, accentuating the large green wreath, accessorized with pinecones and a large, red bow. Tiny, white lights outline the front window and entryway, but we have no other signs of Christmas in sight. I sigh and remind myself I need to put more decorations up for them. They've had way too much going on to even think about decorating for the holidays. Besides, I believe the outside of the house is usually Uncle Joe's job, which means I need to step up and make sure it's taken care of.

I make my way up the front walkway and walk in through the front door, stepping right into the living room. I close the door behind me and look around. Finding no movement, I call out, but not too loud, in case Uncle Joe is resting. "Aunt Vivienne?" I slip my coat off and pull open the closet door. I reach for a hanger and wrap my coat around it before I slip it into the closet and shut the door.

"She went to the store!" I hear Uncle Joe's muffled yell.

It sounds like he's upstairs. He's probably in his room, where Aunt Viv made sure he'd be set up comfortably. At least I know he's awake. Turning around, I immediately jog up the steps, heading towards their bedroom. I hear the sound of the television echoing down the narrow hallway as I stride down the hall, lined with several family pictures, including many with me and continue on to the master bedroom. I step inside to find him propped up with several pillows behind him in his Queen sleigh bed. He has the burgundy floral comforter pulled up to his waist, while he's wearing his dark blue and green flannel pajamas, his curly salt and pepper hair in disarray. "Hey, Uncle Joe," I say, announcing my presence. He looks over at me, his face still slightly pale and drawn as he offers me a small smile. "How are you feeling?" I question, my heart clenching with worry.

He reaches for the remote control and points it at the television, immediately turning it off. Then, he sets it down on the small oak nightstand adorned with antique brass handles, matching the other bedroom furniture. He readjusts slightly, before he looks back at me and responds. "I'm fine, Tyler," he insists. He gives me a firm stare, as if he wants me to see the truth in his blue eyes. He sighs heavily and reaches up, pushing his thick, gray hair off his forehead. "How's the coffee shop?" he inquires, changing the subject. Knowing him, I'm sure he wants to talk about anything except his health.

"It's great," I reply. "Really," I emphasize, attempting to ease his concerns. "Mandy has been wonderful. She has really helped me out with everything," I apprise him. The coffee shop is the last thing he should be worrying about right now. He may not want to talk about his health, but I just want him to focus on getting better.

Uncle Joe nods his head in acknowledgement, with a small smile on his face, as if he's lost in thought. "She's a good egg," he recognizes.

"She misses you. Everyone does," I declare, honestly. I hope it will bring him some comfort knowing everyone has been asking about him, as well as continue to pray for him to heal quickly and feel better. I know I want to see him back to himself again.

He sighs again and concedes, "Yeah, well, I miss all of them, too. If your aunt would only let me get back to work," he begins, trailing off with a grimace and a hopeful look in his eyes.

I shake my head, the corners of my mouth turning up in amusement. Of course, he wants to go back to work already. He's never done well with sitting still for very long, but that can't happen, not yet anyway. "You're not ready, Uncle Joe," I insist. "You know that," I reiterate.

He runs his hand down his face and grunts stubbornly in response. "Yeah, well," he grumbles, unintelligibly.

I pinch my lips tightly together fighting a smile. I think a subject change might help; a topic that has nothing to do with him. "I met the girl from the gallery next door," I apprise him. Noelle's expressive blue eyes and sweet smile, the first thing that comes to my mind.

His eyes widen as he looks at me with interest. Then, he arches his eyebrows and prompts, "You mean, Noelle?"

I nod my head in confirmation and murmur, "Yeah. She sent some gingerbread cookies home for you if Aunt Viv says you can have them," I advise.

"Gingerbread cookies you say? We don't have to tell your aunt everything," he claims, smirking.

"Sorry, Uncle Joe, but after this week, I'll definitely be asking her before I hand them over," I enlighten him.

He grimaces and mumbles, "Well, you can't blame me for trying."

I chuckle and nod my head in agreement. "Noelle invited me to her grand opening tonight," I add, a smile tugging at my lips.

"You should go, Tyler," he urges.

I grimace, suddenly wary to leave Uncle Joe. "I don't know. I'm kind of tired," I mumble. Glancing at him, he gives me a look, telling me he sees right through my lame excuse. "How long have you been here alone?" I prompt.

He purses his lips, annoyed with having so much attention focused on him. "Ty, your aunt just ran out to get some ingredients for her cookies," he notifies me.

"Oh!" I exclaim, a grin instantly spreading across my face. "Her chocolate chip cookies?" I question, my mouth already watering at the thought of them.

He grins, chuckling softly at my reaction. "What else?" he prods playfully, knowing the answer will be obvious to me. Aunt Viv always makes sure we have a good supply of her chocolate chip cookies around the house during the holidays, especially when I'm around.

"Great," I murmur, happily. "I love those," I announce, as if he doesn't already know they're my favorite.

"Well," he begins, "they'll be waiting here for you when you get home," he proclaims.

"I don't know," I mumble, still hesitant to leave. I want to go, but I should be here with him.

"What do you think I'm going to eat them all?" he asks, laughing at his own joke.

I chuckle in response and shake my head in amusement. "No," I reply, knowing he's on a strict diet. "I just feel bad," I admit. "I came here to help you guys out, not to go to a party," I remind him.

He huffs a laugh. Smirking, he states, "Tyler, it hardly sounds like a party. Besides, you're helping us out plenty," he claims. "It's only been a few days. Go to the grand opening," he encourages. "Plus, you can go for both of us."

"Are you sure?" I prod. I still feel unsettled with leaving him and need clarification.

He gives me a firm nod of his head and confidently declares, "Absolutely. Maybe you can meet some new people," he adds. I bite my lower lip in hesitation, trying to decide what the best thing to do would be. "Tyler, let's be realistic," he prompts. "You're going to be here for a while. I'm not going to be able to get back to fully running the coffee shop for at least a few months," he reminds me. "That is, if you're planning on staying that long," he mumbles, backtracking.

They amaze me how they never want to put too much pressure on me to help them with anything. They just need to understand I want to be here to help them. I immediately interrupt him and vow, "That's the plan."

He smiles, nodding his head in acknowledgement as he continues. "Well, since that's the plan and you're going to be here for a while," he reiterates, "don't you think you should get to know Mount Holly a little more and get to know some of the people in it a little better?" he probes, arching his eyebrows in challenge. "Maybe even go out and dare I say it, have some fun?" he teases.

I shrug in response and murmur, "Yeah, I guess." Sighing, I explain, "I just feel like I should be helping you out more."

"You're helping plenty, Ty," he repeats. "And we both know you will be helping out a lot more," he reminds me. "It's going to be a few months before I'm able to go back to work," he mutters.

I huff a laugh and smirk. "Yeah, before Aunt Viv lets you go back to work."

"Yeah, that too," he grumbles and quickly shakes away the thought. "Mount Holly is going to be your home, at least for the next couple months," he reiterates. "So, settle in here, you know?" he prods. "Try to unwind," he proposes.

I nod my head slowly in acceptance. "Yeah," I murmur. I know he's right, but it's still hard to leave when he's barely been home from the hospital. For the same reason, it's also difficult for me to paste a smile on my face to go out to meet people and socialize, even if it is for Noelle's store opening. "Thanks, Uncle Joe," I tell him, sincerely. Even when he's recuperating from a heart attack, he's watching out for me. Sometimes I wonder how he does it all.

"You're welcome," he replies, the corners of his mouth curving up. "Now go set the table before your aunt gets home," he recommends. I chuckle and nod my head in agreement. Then I turn and walk out of his room, making my way back downstairs to do as he asked. After dinner, I'll get myself cleaned up and ready to go out. I must admit, I am looking forward to seeing Noelle again. Plus, I'll be able to see her in her element. I smile to myself as I walk into the kitchen wondering what tonight will be like.

Chapter 4

Noelle

It feels as if only a few minutes have passed when I'm putting the finishing touches on my painting. I take a step back to assess my work. I gasp, suddenly startled at the sound of a loud banging, my hand falling to my chest to calm my wildly beating heart. I instantly realize it's coming from the front door, so I set my paintbrush down and quickly pull off my smock. I set it down on an empty spot on the shelves, before I rush out of my art studio and into the front of the shop. "I'm coming!" I yell, hurrying to the door. Noticing Daphne on the other side of the glass, I swiftly unlock the door to let her in, my eyebrows drawn down in concern.

I barely have the door unlocked, when she frantically yanks it open, instantly breathing a heavy sigh of relief as her eyes land on me. "Oh, thank goodness!" she exclaims. She immediately closes the distance between us and wraps me up in a tight hug, causing my own anxiety to skyrocket.

"Daphne!" I exclaim, uneasily as I hug her back. "What's wrong?" I ask.

She steps back, holding onto my shoulders and looks at me with wide eyes, her eyebrows nearly reaching her hairline. "What's wrong?" she repeats, as if I lost my mind. "It's six-fifteen!" she announces, with blatant exasperation.

"What?" I inquire, not sure I heard her right. I glance at her clothes and hair, suddenly noticing how stunning she looks. She's wearing a beautiful A-line, satin dress, with thin black and gray horizontal stripes and patterned bunches of flowers in rosy pinks, whites and shades of gray. The crew neckline has a thick strip of black, clipped at her nape. She accented her dress with a flowing, black cardigan sweater and her favorite, short, black, suede boots with a one and a half inch heel. Her hair falls softly over her right shoulder, with a slight wave at the ends, while she has her make-up done up perfectly. She's already dressed for the opening tonight...my thoughts trail off at the realization. "My opening," I grumble.

"I've been trying to call you for the past hour and a half!" she declares accusingly.

I wince, feeling guilty and slightly panicked at the same time. I pull my phone out of my back pocket and the screen instantly lights up, filling up with several notifications. "No!" I complain. "It was on silent," I groan, suddenly aware. I know I don't like to be disrupted when I'm working on a project, but I know better on a night like tonight to completely disconnect from the outside world. I can't believe I did that! I quickly scroll through the notifications, seeing numerous missed calls and messages, mostly from Daphne and my family. "I've got missed calls from you, Jackie, Mom, Dad..." I grimace, trailing off as I go through my messages. I groan in frustration as complete understanding sets in. "I missed dinner!" I exclaim.

Daphne grimaces, giving me a look full of empathy as she nods her head in verification. "You sure did. When we couldn't find you, we all went looking," she enlightens me.

I wince, feeling guilty for making them all worry. "I'm so sorry. I lost all track of time," I explain.

She arches her eyebrows in question and probes, "Painting again?"

I offer her a tight smile and nod my head in confirmation. "Yes," I admit, regretfully. "I'm so sorry," I repeat my apology.

She nods her head in understanding. It's not like this is the first time I've lost track of time while creating something. "I probably should've known and looked here first," she concedes. "Go home, get dressed and get back here," she instructs. "I'll set everything else up for you," she offers.

"You're the best," I proclaim. "My family is going to kill me," I whine, in anticipation.

Daphne pulls out her phone and quickly begins typing. "We have a group text going," she tells me. "I'll tell them you're okay and you're on your way home."

I breathe a sigh of relief, but I still have to hurry if I'm going to make it back here on time. I rush back to the counter, swiping my olive-green winter coat off the chair behind it and pull it on. "Thank you! I owe you, Daph!" I yell.

She smirks. "Yeah, I'll put it on your tab," she teases.

Then she places her hands gently on my back and nearly pushes me out the front door making me laugh. "I'm going," I declare.

I wave and begin running down the block, passing the small shops in town, now brightly lit with Christmas lights and decorations including wreaths, Christmas trees, and windows with scenes portraying things like the North Pole, a winter wonderland or a family on Christmas morning. So much more seems to be decorated than what I saw the other night. Some shops have all white lights, while some have all red, green, or blue, as well as several with a rainbow of colored lights. I enter my neighborhood, noticing there's a wreath on nearly every front door, the colors becoming a blur as I hurry home. Some houses have almost everything decorated for Christmas, while other houses keep their decorations much more simple. I turn onto my street and keep running until I reach my house. Then, I dash up the steep blacktop driveway, to my white, colonial house, with black roof and shutters, sitting at the top of a small hill.

Mom and dad decorated the outside of our house for Christmas, using all white lights. They have them adorning the bushes and trees, as well as hanging underneath the front windows. Garland wrapped with white lights hang around the front door, along the railing on the front porch, as well as around the garage. Two large red and white twisted candy canes decorate the sides of the garage, a large brightly lit snowman with a top hat and red Christmas bow tie, sits just off to the side of the garage. I push through the front door, adorned with a pine Christmas wreath, wrapped with a thick, red and gold, Christmas ribbon, tied with an elaborate bow. I step into the house and kick off my shoes as I call out, "Mom? Dad?"

"Look who decided to show up," my younger brother, Dylan murmurs sarcastically, startling me. I spin around to find him sitting in the wooden chair in the corner, right by the front door, a slight smirk playing on his lips. He barely glances up at me, before looking down at the phone in his hand and continues mindlessly scrolling through it. He's all dressed up for my grand opening and waiting for me. He's wearing tan dress pants, a pale pink, button-down shirt and a gray, pink and white striped tie. He runs his fingers through his brown hair, slightly longer on top, pushing it out of his eyes and letting it flop over to his left. He looks more like our dad, while I look more like my mom, but we both have the same blue eyes.

I narrow my eyes at him and snap, "Put a sock in it, Dylan."

He shakes his head at me, still smirking in amusement. "You are in so much trouble," he taunts, glancing up to see my reaction. He loves giving me a hard time.

My mom rushes into the foyer, her straight chestnut, reddish-brown hair styled perfectly, ending just above her shoulders. She's wearing a beautiful, fitted crepe silk, dark burgundy dress with the scoop neck falling in loose layers, paired with simple black pumps. "Noelle!" she exclaims, the moment she sees me. "Where have you been?" she questions. I flinch hearing both the anxiety and relief in the sound of her voice.

"In my studio," I inform her, regretful. "Painting," I mumble and wince, as guilt suddenly overwhelms me again.

She immediately pulls me into a tight hug, and I wrap my arms around her reflexively. "We thought something happened to you," she adds, sounding choked up. "Your father is at the hospital searching the Emergency Room," she enlightens me.

I flinch at her news, my stomach twisting into knots, knowing how concerned they were about me. "I know. I'm so sorry. I started painting and I lost track of time," I explain, weakly.

"We were so worried," mom emphasizes. "I don't know if I should hug you or hang you," she grumbles, giving me a stern look of warning, the same look I still cower away from.

My brother raises his hand without lifting his head or his gaze and announces, "I vote hang."

My mom finally lets me go and turns towards my brother, giving him the same look of warning, she just gave me. "Dylan," she scolds, firmly. He barely glances at her and shrugs his shoulders in response.

My mom shakes her head and releases a heavy sigh, letting it go, knowing we have very little time. She turns her attention back to me, her hands resting on my shoulders. "You better go get ready," she reminds me.

I nod in agreement and mumble, "I know. I know. Fifteen minutes," I inform her.

She arches her eyebrows in challenge and declares, "You have ten."

"But..." I open my mouth to argue.

She shakes her head and immediately interrupts me. "You can't be late to your own grand opening," she contends, leaving no room for argument.

I heave a sigh, knowing she's right, but I hate that I put myself in this position again, especially tonight. "Right," I grumble, scrunching up my face, frustrated with myself. "Ten minutes," I confirm, relenting, hoping I can make it happen.

Dylan mumbles sarcastically, under his breath, "Like that'll happen." He looks up at mom, knowing she's giving him another disparaging look. "What?" he prompts, innocently. She shakes her head in disbelief and walks away from both of us without saying another word.

I turn and race up the stairs, taking them two at a time. I run into the bathroom and quickly wash my face, brush my teeth and reapply my basic make-up. I pull my hair out of the messy bun and quickly run a brush through it. I glance in the mirror, looking at my reflection. I shrug, thankful it doesn't look too bad. I put on some fresh deodorant before I carefully slip my dress on over my head. "I'm glad I decided what I wanted to wear earlier today," I mumble to myself. I never would've been ready otherwise. Then I grab my glass bottle of perfume and lightly spritz it on my neck before setting it back on the bathroom counter.

I stride back into my room and stop in front of my full-length mirror. I assess my reflection as I slip on my simple, black, patent leather shoes. The rose pink, ribbed dress falls a few inches above my knees. The sleeves stop at three-quarters in length, with a cutout at the top, leaving my shoulders bare. The neckline comes down in a V in front with ribbons of fabric crisscrossing, as if it's tied together at the bottom of the V. It's simple, but also unique and classy. I think it's absolutely perfect for tonight; at least I hope so.

I glance at the time on my phone and grimace. I don't really have time, but I really want to talk to my grandmother before I go. I bite my lower lip nervously as I scroll through recent calls and tap my grandma's name before I change my mind. She picks up almost immediately. "Hello?" she answers. I smile to myself, feeling a little more relaxed already, as I picture her sitting in her old tan leather chair with her short blonde hair with shades of gray looking as if she just brushed it, and her blue eyes mirroring my own as she talks into the telephone I know is still plugged into the wall.

"Hi Grandma! It's Noelle," I announce, my smile growing at the sound of her voice.

"Noelle!" she happily exclaims. "How nice to hear from you! Are you ready for your big night tonight?" she inquires.

"Just about," I reply.

"How do you feel?" she questions.

I grimace and admit, "I'm really nervous."

She laughs and concedes, "So am I!"

I take a deep breath and anxiously blurt out what I've been thinking. "I have everything riding on this, Gram," I divulge.

She sighs heavily and gently acknowledges, "I know you do, Honey. It's a big leap of faith," she proclaims.

"I'm so thankful that mom and dad let me move back home, until I get my shop off the ground," I confess. "They have really been incredible throughout this entire journey," I add.

"Noelle, you are their eldest child," she emphasizes. "You are setting an example for Jackie and Dylan."

I bite my bottom lip and slowly release it as I contemplate her words. "Do you really think so?" I prompt.

"I know so," she confirms, with complete confidence. "You are a dream chaser, Noelle. You are showing your brother and sister, and everyone else for that matter, that people are able to catch the dreams they chase if they try hard enough," she declares, encouraging me.

I smile to myself as I feel my whole body relax with her words. "Thanks, Grandma," I murmur, gratefully.

"You better go, honey," she states, reminding me of the time. "Your public awaits," she adds playfully, chuckling softly.

"I love you," I tell her.

"I love you too, Noelle," she replies, sweetly.

"I wish you were here," I claim, sincerely. My heart clenches briefly, missing her. "Bye, Grandma."

"Goodbye," she responds. I hear the phone banging around as she returns it to the cradle to hang it up, just as I tap end on my phone.

I glance in the mirror one more time, wanting one last look at my appearance. I take a deep breath and exhale slowly. "Here goes nothing," I mumble to myself in encouragement.

I walk out my bedroom door and downstairs, just as my dad strides in through the back door, returning from the hospital. He's dressed in tan dress slacks, a dark blue, long-sleeved sweater with a collar and two dark brown buttons at the neck, the top one undone. His short, brown hair appears as if he's been running his fingers through it from nerves, causing me to feel even worse.

He instantly closes the distance between us and wraps his arms around me and I relax into his embrace, my arms going around his back. I hear his heavy sigh of relief as he gives me a tight squeeze. "I'm so glad you're safe," he whispers, hoarsely. He takes a step back and holds me out at arms length. He narrows his eyes and gives me a stern look in caution. "Call us next time!" he demands vehemently.

"I'm sorry, Dad," I apologize. "I promise, I will," I claim.

He nods his head in acknowledgement. Then he forces a smile and insists, "We can talk more later. It's time to go."

I nervously clasp my hands together. Then I turn and make my way to the front closet to grab my winter coat on our way out the door. I can do this.

Chapter 5

Noelle

I push through the front door of The First Noelle, with my mom, my dad and my brother, Dylan in tow. We step inside finding Daphne and my sister, Jackie already in the main room, adding a few finishing touches to the grand opening decorations. They're enhancing the atmosphere by adding more Christmas decorations to help the shop look even more festive for the celebration tonight, as well as ready for the holidays. The moment Jackie sees us, she drops the green Christmas garland she's holding in her hands and swiftly strides over to me. "Noelle," she exclaims, with a bright smile on her face. Then she crashes into me, causing an involuntary rush of air to exit my lungs as she throws her arms around me and hugs me tightly.

I grab onto her elbows to regain my balance and then I gratefully return her embrace as I catch my breath. "Hey, Jackie!" I reply. She's dressed in a simple, but classy, gray sweater dress, paired with black, ankle-high boots with a two-inch heel, bringing her a little closer to my height. She has her golden blonde hair styled beautifully, with loose curls hanging down just over her shoulders. She has the same blue eyes and broad smile as both Dylan and me, but she has more of a heart-shaped face with her high cheekbones and button nose. It's always been completely obvious to most people that we're sisters, although she's four years younger than me.

"I thought something happened to you," she reiterates the same comment I've been hearing all night. She finally steps back and releases me, as she narrows her eyes at me in accusation. Then she gives me the same

47

threatening look I get from mom. I want to roll my eyes, but I don't. I feel like I can't really blame her. I would be the same way, if we were all trying to reach her all day, but we couldn't get in touch with her. To be fair, though, I am usually the one disappearing for long periods of time, skipping meals or losing sleep and most of the time, they know where to find me. I really don't do it on purpose. It's just that once I start a project, my brain won't let me stop until I get to a certain point. Many times, that point for me will be when I finish the project or I'm at least close to it and I know that can take a while depending on the project. I just have to remember to leave my ringer on next time.

I sigh heavily as I take a step back from her. I grimace and offer her an apologetic smile. "I know. I'm sorry," I mumble, regretfully again. It feels as if my apology should just be on repeat, but what else can I do now? I really do feel terrible that everyone was so worried about me.

"I saw the painting," she apprises me, with a bright smile. "It's great," she compliments, looking into my eyes and letting her sincerity shine through.

"Thanks," I reply, appreciatively. I don't think I'll ever tire of hearing someone tell me they like something I created, especially when it's someone from my family; the pride I feel can be overwhelming. Maybe they're not always the best judge of my work, but I believe their impressions or opinions still probably have the biggest impact on me. I know I shouldn't depend on them for my confidence, and I don't, but I'm grateful to know they will always be there to support me. I really couldn't ask for anything more. Although, I do wish I could pull that confidence in by myself. I feel such a strong connection to everything I create, and I believe it shows in my work. I'm really proud of it, but at the same time, I still have my doubts when it comes to sharing it with other people. I guess it makes me feel completely vulnerable. That thought terrifies me, especially because I'm about to open the doors to my shop for the first time. I need a boost of confidence quickly because it seems I'm not quite there yet and I need my confidence to shine through, especially now.

"Are you going to hang it out here?" she inquires. She scans the room quickly before returning her gaze to mine.

I shrug, not quite sure what I want to do with it yet. "Maybe," I murmur. "Not tonight, though. It's still wet," I add as an explanation.

She nods in understanding, as my mom steps up between the two of us and interrupts. "Can I see it?" Mom requests.

"Sure," I respond, nodding in agreement. "We can leave our coats back there, too," I suggest, loud enough for Dad and Dylan to hear me too.

"Doors open in ten minutes," Daphne advises.

"Thanks, Daph," I convey and offer her a grateful smile.

She grins, murmuring, "I'm happy to help."

I hold out my hand, gesturing towards the back of the shop. "It's in the back on the left," I advise my family. Jackie wanders back towards the display table to finish hanging the garland she dropped to the floor, as I follow the rest of my family towards the back of the store and my make-shift art studio. I'll make it more permanent soon. I just need to put a few more things away, so everything feels more organized. As I reach the doorway, I spin back towards them with a smile. "Let me put your coats in here," I offer. I hold out my hands and wait for them to hand them over.

Dad, Mom and Dylan all quickly slip out of their jackets and then give them to me, one by one. I step into my art studio and set them down on a clean, empty shelf. I watch as my mom and dad look all around them, taking in my paintings and other artwork. A small, satisfied smile lights up my face and causes my heart to overflow with pride, as I overhear their murmured comments of praise.

Dylan turns around and suddenly stops in his tracks, noticing the painting I got lost in today. The same painting that caused me to be so late getting home tonight. With a wide-eyed glance in my direction, he gestures towards the painting, still sitting and drying on the black, wooden easel, just outside my studio. "Is this the painting?" he probes.

"Yup," I confirm, popping the p. I step up next to him and cross my arms over my chest. I can't stop myself from taking it in, assessing the brushstrokes and critiquing my own work. "What do you think?" I inquire, biting my lower lip anxiously before releasing it. I glance in his direction out of the corner of my eye and back at the painting in front of us attempting to see what he might see.

His eyes widen even further as he arches his eyebrows in pure disbelief. Then, he purses his lips and states the obvious, "They're cookies." I fight a wince as Dad lightly smacks Dylan in the back of the head, causing him to flinch in response and rub the back of his head.

I pinch my lips tightly together and nod slowly in confirmation. I paste a smile on my face, before I elaborate, "Chocolate chip cookies."

Mom glances at Dylan out of the corner of her eye and immediately steps in, anticipating his reaction. Like always, she wants to do what she can to encourage me. "It's great, Noelle," she praises with a broad smile.

"What's so great about a painting of cookies?" Dylan inquires, his confusion obvious in the tone of his voice.

"Dylan," Dad states firmly, his tone, scolding. He points Dylan towards the exit and tilts his head down towards him, giving him a look of warning.

His eyes widen and he innocently questions, "What did I do?" I'd probably laugh at his reaction if I wasn't so nervous about the opening tonight, but my stomach won't stop churning as if I'm on a never-ending tilt-a-whirl.

Dad ignores Dylan's question, pressing his lips tightly together and giving a slight shake of his head, hoping it's enough to discourage him. Mom reiterates her compliment, bringing my attention back to her. "It's a very nice painting, Noelle," she emphasizes, as only a mom can do. I smile politely in response.

"Of cookies," Dylan repeats, deadpan.

"Dylan, out!" Dad firmly demands, pointing towards the front of the store. Dylan's eyes widen in surprise, but he remains frozen. Dad steps towards him and grabs him by his tie. He gives it a light tug and leads him out into the front of the shop, as he softly reprimands him. "If you're not mature enough to handle an art show," he grumbles, his voice trailing off as they walk further away.

I pinch my lips tightly together in attempt to suppress my laughter. I finally release a real smile and chuckle softly feeling some of my tension ease out of me. I shake my head, wondering if I had been that bad when I was in high school, but I quickly shake the idea off. There's no way I was as difficult as my brother. I busy myself by putting a few stray items away in the closet, trying not to think about what he said. I don't want to let his opinion bother me, especially with the doors of my new store about to open.

I feel my mom step a little closer to me before she speaks. "Dylan doesn't know what he's talking about, Noelle," Mom claims, sweetly, in attempt to comfort me.

I smirk, the corners of my mouth twitching up in amusement. "It's fine, Mom. He's seventeen," I mumble, as if that explains everything. Maybe I'm trying to convince myself not to believe him by saying it out loud, but sometimes I can't stop myself from listening to any words encouraging my doubt. It doesn't matter if I know better. When the words come from someone I'm close to, even Dylan, I tend to find them especially hurtful, but I quickly cover it up, attempting to hide my concern and my fears that I'm not good enough.

I watch as my mom tilts her head to the side, while she considers my painting. The cookies are piled atop a round, white platter, with the edge of the plate accented with green Christmas holly adorned with red berries. Then, behind the plate, I painted shades of light blue and whites, making it appear as if they're sitting on a tablecloth and maintaining the focus on the cookies, not the background. I do realize it's a simple painting, but it was the perfect thing for me to paint to be able to try a few different techniques with my new paintbrush. As long as I put my heart into my work, that's what matters to me. At least that's what I'm going to keep reminding myself.

"I bet you could sell it to the bakery or Cuppa' Joe," she suggests. I smile up at her; thankful she's my mom. She always seems to say just the right thing, at exactly the right time. She helps boost my confidence, without even realizing it. Then again, isn't that what moms are supposed to do? But I know everyone isn't as lucky as me and either way, I'm grateful.

Glancing at the painting one more time, I get an anxious feeling in my gut. I love doing all my artwork, especially painting, but I'm not sure how other people will really feel about it and that's what scares me. I glance around me, taking everything in. I've put so much money and heart into this place, but now that the doors are about to open, my stomach won't stop churning. I honestly wonder if people will spend money on what I create, if they will want to. Plus, so much of my art is very personal to me. I want to do well, but to do that I have to let go of a piece of me every time I'm able to sell something. Will I be able to do that when the time comes? I bite my lower lip anxiously and release it slowly, dragging it through my teeth. I guess I'll be finding out soon enough, one way or another.

I take a deep, calming breath and shrug my shoulders, noncommittally. "Maybe. It won't be fully dry for a day or two anyway. I'll hang it then," I divulge. I really don't want to get into the small details right now, anyway. I have other things to think about tonight.

She grins and gives me an encouraging nod of approval. "You should," she emphasizes. She pauses and then reiterates, "It's a fantastic painting."

I laugh, enjoying mom's continuous praise, even if I do believe she's exaggerating. At least I know someone will always love all my work, or at least claim they do. "I don't know about fantastic, Mom," I mutter, the corners of my mouth still twitching up in amusement. "I was trying out a paintbrush Daphne gave me," I explain.

"Oh, that's sweet," she concurs.

I nod my head in agreement and open my mouth to respond, when the sound of Daphne's voice causes me to pause. She calls out from the front of the shop, loud enough for all of us to hear, "Doors are opening in five minutes!"

At her announcement, my nerves suddenly feel like they're about to get the best of me, swirling around in my stomach like a hurricane. I take a deep breath, trying to calm myself down. I feel a little shaky, although I don't think I look it. I close my eyes and take another deep breath, before exhaling slowly and repeating the process one more time. My heartbeat finally begins slowing down, with my controlled breathing. "Here we go," I mumble, under my breath, feigning confidence. I want to put on a brave face for my mom and dad, and everyone else for that matter, even though my insides feel as if they're about to erupt. I'm proud of my work, just like everyone here with me in this moment. Now it's time to share it with the rest of the world and doing that makes me feel completely exposed. It's like sharing every part of me, inside and out, for everyone to see. Every piece is a part of who I am. I take one more deep breath and reiterate inaudibly to myself, "I've got this."

I paste a smile on my face, hoping the rest of me will follow suit. Then, I follow my mom towards the front of my new store on shaky legs. I take another deep breath and exhale slowly as I prepare to open the front door of "The First Noelle" for the first time. My stomach continues twisting like a tornado. I hear my blood rushing in my ears, the only sound I'm able to register. I close my eyes and take one more deep breath, attempting to control my anxiety one more time, before the door opens. "I can do this," I reiterate. I open my eyes, square my shoulders and faking self-assurance I announce, "Okay, I'm ready." I feel Daphne's and my family's eyes all on me. Knowing they're all here to support me means everything to me. I just need to keep remembering that for the rest of the night and I'll be just fine. My focus remains on the glass front door and who might walk through it tonight. No matter what, I'm grateful to every single one of them...I think.

Chapter 6

Noelle

I smile wide and welcome two tall, thin, beautiful women, fashionably dressed, one with long, blonde hair and soft blue eyes and the other with long, dark brown hair and coffee brown eyes as they enter my shop. People have been going in and out all night, complimenting me on my work, spending time looking around and even buying some of my things. I almost can't believe my dream is coming true. Everything about this feels surreal. "Thank you so much for coming tonight," I express to both women. They return my smile and I gesture for them to go on, and explore further into the shop. "Take a look around and enjoy some cookies and hot cocoa," I suggest. "Please, let me know if you have any questions," I add.

They both nod in acknowledgement and politely murmur, "Thank you." As they continue looking around the shop, I greet the next couple, followed by a family and another couple. I continue welcoming guests and answering questions about my artwork, thrilled with every new face that passes over the threshold making me almost giddy.

During a brief moment of respite, I quietly slip out the back door, needing a moment to myself in the fresh air. The whole night is beginning to feel a little bit overwhelming. It nearly doesn't seem real. I take a deep breath and almost immediately regret not grabbing my coat, as the cold air burns my lungs and goosebumps prickle my skin. I shouldn't stay out here too long though, anyway. I should be fine.

I walk across the alley and sit down on the black metal stairs going up the side of the brick building, thinking about all the people who have been going in and out of my store all night, including friends, family and neighbors. Plus, there have been so many people here I don't know. I think that's what pushes me over the proverbial edge and makes me wonder how all of them found out about my opening. I advertised for it, but I kept all my marketing relatively local and I'm pretty sure I know almost everyone in Mount Holly. I'm not sure how it happened, but I'm thankful and truly ecstatic tonight seems to be going so well.

I hear one of the shop doors open and then close behind me with a click, followed by the light click of heels against the pavement. Daphne rounds the end of the stairs and rushes up to me, her eyes wide with excitement, causing me to smile in anticipation. "Noelle!" she exclaims, elated. "Noelle, what are you doing out here? I've been looking for you," she conveys.

"I just needed a little bit of fresh air," I answer, the corners of my mouth lifting upwards at her animation.

She nods in understanding and then her smile grows, as she sits down next to me on the stairs. "Guess what?" she prompts bouncing on her toes, but she doesn't wait for me to answer. "There's a man here from New York City that wants to buy one of your paintings," she enlightens me, her eyes sparking with pride.

My mouth drops open and I gasp. "What?" I question, my eyes wide in surprise. "You're joking," I mumble, with clear disbelief.

She shakes her head and full of delight proclaims, "No!"

"Which one?" I question.

She tilts her head to the side and scrunches her eyebrows together, as if she's trying to recall. "I don't know," she begins. "He's wearing a suit and he's got brown hair," she mumbles, describing the man.

I chuckle softly and shake my head. "No, I mean which painting?" I prod for clarification.

"Oh, ah," she mumbles, thinking. Finally, she shrugs her shoulders and admits, "I don't know. I think it has a tree on a road or something," she mumbles, vaguely.

My eyes widen, as a sudden wave of panic washes over me. "Daph!" I exclaim. "I wasn't going to sell that one," I announce.

Her eyebrows scrunch together in confusion. She probes, "Why not?"

I briefly pinch my lips tightly together, attempting to come up with how to explain my reasoning to her. "I don't know," I murmur, softly. "I really like it," I finally admit. Some of my paintings are just going to be extremely difficult to let go.

Her eyebrows shoot up to her hairline. "So," she begins, dragging out the word, "you're only going to sell the paintings you don't like?" she probes, in challenge.

"Well, no…I…um…" I stammer, awkwardly. I release a heavy sigh, knowing she's right.

She grins and gives her head a slight shake in amusement. Then she grabs my hand and pulls me up. "Come on, silly," she murmurs. "Come on," she repeats as she tugs me back inside and I reluctantly trail along right behind her.

Daphne walks me right over to the man standing in front of my painting, admiring it. He seems to be a very professional looking man, wearing a long, black dress overcoat, over a light blue dress shirt and matching tie in a darker shade of blue. He's about the same height as me with brown hair, long enough to run his fingers through it, but trimmed short and neat. He turns towards us with a friendly smile as we approach, his brown eyes meeting mine through his dark-rimmed glasses.

I attempt to gulp down the lump in my throat as Daphne introduces me. "This is the artist," she announces, "Noelle Palmer."

He extends his hand out to me in greeting. "Miss Palmer, it truly is a pleasure," he claims. I place my hand in his, and he shakes my hand firmly.

"It's nice to meet you, Mister," I trail off, not knowing his name, as I release his hand.

"Carlyle. John Carlyle," he clarifies.

I smile, politely, still feeling my nerves swarming in my stomach. "Mr. Carlyle. Daphne tells me that you're interested in one of my paintings," I convey.

He nods in affirmation. "Correct. This one," he happily states. He points to a small painting of a tree beside a hilly road.

"Interesting," I murmur, as my stomach does a flip-flop. I nod slowly in acknowledgement as I glance between him and the painting. "May I ask, why this particular painting?" I probe.

He looks at me and his eyes suddenly go soft, as if he's remembering something close to his heart. He smiles as if he has no choice, but to do so and gives me a slight nod in agreement. Rocking back on his heels, he admits, "It reminds me of the entrance to Evergreen Mountain Ski Resort."

I grin and compliment him. "Good eye. It is," I confirm.

His smile broadens and he nearly bounces on his feet in enthusiasm. "I knew it! I knew it!" he exclaims. "I have to have this painting," he insists.

I wince and quickly apologize, "I'm sorry, Mr. Carlyle, but I wasn't planning on selling this one."

Daphne hits me lightly from behind, but I refuse to turn around and look at her. I know exactly what she would

58

say to me right now. I paste an apologetic smile on my face and try to maintain my focus on Mr. Carlyle.

"You don't understand. Please, sell it to me," he pleads with me. "My wife would absolutely adore it," he claims.

"Really?" I question. The way he says that makes me feel like there's more to his story, piquing my curiosity.

His expression turns regretful as he sighs. He glances at me and attempts to explain. "I haven't gotten anything for her for Christmas yet. We go up to ski at Evergreen every winter. I proposed to her right in front of that tree," he pauses and points to the tree in the painting for emphasis, "twenty-five years ago," he finishes, his love for his wife shining through.

"Awe," Daphne croons.

"I wouldn't even know how to price it," I tell him, honestly. I didn't know where to begin on pricing my paintings because of how personal they are to me. It makes it much harder to part with something like that. I had only priced some of the paintings I had on display tonight and that took me long enough. I didn't think anyone would ask about the ones that didn't have price tags on them.

He looks back at the painting and grins. "I'll give you one thousand dollars for it," he proposes, without looking back at me.

"Dollars?" Daphne questions, her voice squeaking with disbelief.

My eyes widen in surprise. I ask, barely above a whisper, "Excuse me?"

He grimaces and immediately apologizes. "I'm sorry. I didn't mean to offend you," he tells me. "Twenty-five hundred?" he suggests.

Daphne's mouth drops open in astonishment. "What?" she prods, completely stunned.

"Mr. Carlyle, I don't..." I begin, shaking my head.

He immediately cuts me off, "Three thousand dollars, but that's as high as I can go, he declares. "That is all the cash I have on me," he explains.

"Cash?" Daphne repeats. I glance at her out of the corner of my eye, her reaction mirroring mine with wide eyes and her face slightly pale.

"Three thousand dollars for this painting?" I clarify. "This little painting?" I reiterate.

He nods and stares back at the small painting in admiration. "I can see the detail, as small as it is. I'm sure it took you a long time to create such a unique painting. It's exquisite," he adds.

"I don't know what to say," I mumble, dumbfounded.

Daphne suddenly gets her voice back and steps between us, sticking her hand out towards Mr. Carlyle. "I do," she proclaims. "Sold!" she happily announces, as he takes her hand and shakes it firmly. His smile widens with Daphne's words. "Come with me and I will ring you up," she instructs.

Mr. Carlyle releases Daphne's hand and turns towards me, grinning ear to ear. He grabs my hand and shakes it vigorously in both joy and elation. "Thank you. Thank you, Miss Palmer." He pauses before announcing, I think we could do some work together."

My eyebrows draw down in confusion. Did I miss something while I was processing this? "What do you mean?" I inquire.

He chuckles and mumbles to himself as a reminder, "I'm in Vermont." He gives his head a light shake and then explains. "You probably don't know who I am. I own a couple of hotels in Manhattan. I would love to talk about commissioning you to have some of your artwork hanging in their lobbies," he enlightens me.

I gasp, completely taken aback. "Wow. Thank you," I murmur, a little overwhelmed.

He reaches into his pocket and pulls out a business card. "I'll leave my card with your assistant," he informs me. "Merry Christmas!"

"Merry Christmas!" I echo, slightly stunned.

"Right this way, Mr. Carlyle," Daphne prompts, gesturing in the direction of the cash register. He smiles and nods in acknowledgement, as he follows her to the front of the store.

I stand in shock for a moment, watching them walk away. I feel a light tap on my arm forcing me to tear my gaze away from them and turn my attention towards a friend of my mom's standing behind me. I take a deep breath and paste a smile on my face as I turn to her. "I love your store. Your work is beautiful, Noelle," she compliments me.

"Thank you," I reply. "Let me know if you have any questions," I advise. Then, I turn to greet more customers. A few minutes later, I'm talking to a woman in a classic black dress with her beautiful five-year-old daughter. The little girl has dark, long, curly hair with big brown eyes, long eyelashes and a contagious sweet smile. She's wearing an adorable dress with black velvet on top and royal blue with a black lined pattern on the skirt.

Daphne steps up to me while I'm talking with them and politely interrupts us. "Excuse me, Noelle?"

I turn towards her and question, "What's up, Daph?"

"Do you have any more earrings?" she asks, hopeful. She bites her bottom lip in anticipation.

"Just the pairs that were on display," I answer.

She grimaces slightly and prods, "None in the back?"

I shake my head and confirm, "None that are finished."

She sighs in defeat and then pushes her shoulders back. "Okay," she answers and nods in acceptance. "Then you're out," she announces.

"I'm out of earrings?" I reiterate, slightly taken aback. There's no way. I thought I made more than enough for one night. "I made two dozen pairs," I reiterate.

Daphne nods in acknowledgement and reaffirms, "You're out."

My mouth drops slightly open in shock as Daphne spins on her heels and strides back towards the customer she was helping. I take a deep breath and turn back towards the woman and her daughter. "I'm sorry, but I have to take care of something," I inform them, apologetically. I smile down at the little girl and hand her a red and white striped candy cane. "This is for you," I offer.

She smiles brightly up at me, as she accepts it, wrapping her little fingers around it. She twists back and forth, her skirt swishing around her as she glances up at me from underneath her long, dark lashes. "Thank you," she murmurs sweetly.

I grin back at them and express, "Thank you for coming."

I quickly stride towards Daphne and the customer standing near the counter, overhearing him as I approach. "It's such a shame. My daughter would have loved a pair of these for Christmas," he concedes.

"I'm so sorry," Daphne apologizes. "I don't know when another pair will become available," she notifies him.

"Tomorrow morning," I announce, as I step between them.

"Noelle!" he exclaims. My eyes widen in surprise at the sight of Professor Shaw standing in my shop. He's a very handsome man, maybe a few years older than my dad. He's about six feet tall with perfectly styled gray hair and toffee brown eyes. He's dressed nicely in a dark navy suit, light blue shirt and thick, striped blue tie. "I'm so proud of you!" he proclaims, fondly.

He holds his arms out to me and I step into them, happily embracing him in greeting. "It's so good to see you, Professor Shaw," I declare. Then, I take a step back to look at him again, letting my mind catch up with reality. I'm so grateful he's here. "I didn't expect you to come all the way from Rhode Island for this," I proclaim, smiling broadly.

"Are you kidding?" he prods, with incredulity. "And miss my star student's grand opening?" he prods. "Never!" he affirms.

"Wait!" Daphne requests. She looks curiously back and forth between the two of us. "You two know each other?" she inquires.

I nod in confirmation and introduce her. "Daphne, this is Professor Shaw. He was my favorite professor at the Art Conservatory," I enlighten her.

"And this is my favorite student," Professor Shaw adds, kindly. He holds his hand out to Daphne and they shake.

"This is my best friend, Daphne," I inform him, gesturing towards her. "She's been my biggest supporter of opening The First Noelle, outside of my family," I admit.

He grins and exclaims, "How wonderful!"

"I can have a pair of earrings finished for you by eleven tomorrow morning," I offer.

"That would be great," he confirms. "I'll check out of my hotel and come right over."

"Great! Any particular colors or style?" I prompt.

He tilts his head to the side, appearing thoughtful. "It's for my sixteen-year-old daughter, so something silver, sparkly and sweet," he explains.

"You got it," I confirm. "I have to leave by noon for my brother's hockey game," I explain, letting him know I have somewhere to be. I don't want to worry about being late.

"No problem," he agrees. "I'll be here right around eleven," he states.

"Thank you," I tell him, appreciatively.

"How much?" he questions.

I huff a laugh. "I'm not charging you for them." He's done so much for me. I honestly don't know if I would have opened this store if he weren't such a wonderful teacher.

"Noelle, that is no way to run a business," he reminds me.

"You came all the way from Rhode Island!" I reiterate.

"So what?" he challenges. Then he turns to Daphne and repeats, "How much for the earrings, Daphne?"

"Fifty dollars," she announces.

"Fifty?" I question, shocked.

"Sold," Professor Shaw declares, ignoring me.

Daphne smiles and informs him, "I'll meet you at the register."

"Ok," he agrees. Then he smiles at me and proclaims, "I'll see you tomorrow, Noelle." Then he turns and heads towards the register to wait for Daphne to pay.

Daphne takes a deep breath, holding up her hands in defense and immediately begins to explain. "Okay, I know what you're going to say," she begins, trailing off.

I instantly interrupt, challenging her, "Fifty dollars per pair, Daphne?"

She shrugs like it's no big deal. "We sold the first dozen within ten minutes of opening the store, so we raised the price from thirty dollars to..."

I cut her off again, "Fifty? Are you crazy?" I prod, incredulously.

"It's called supply and demand," she insists. "Just think about it. You're going to have to start from scratch just to keep your customers," she justifies.

I pinch my lips tightly together and look around the shop, trying to take a quick mental inventory. I suddenly realize how much is really gone. I slowly turn back to her and relent, mumbling, "I never thought about it like that.

"Well, you need to start," she asserts. Then she spins on her heel and strides back towards the register and Professor Shaw. Just then, one of my friends from high school waves as she steps inside the shop. She immediately makes her way directly to me, not giving me the chance to think anymore about tonight's sales or Daphne's words, for now anyway.

Chapter 7

Tyler

"Get some rest, Uncle Joe," I advise. I'm relieved he's finally looking so much better, but he still appears incredibly tired. I don't want him to push himself too hard or too fast. It's not worth the risk.

He gives me a weary smile. "I'm fine, Tyler," he maintains. I nod my head in acknowledgement. "Go to Noelle's opening," he encourages, again. "Someone needs to be there from our family to welcome her and congratulate her on opening her new shop," he reminds me.

"I'm going," I claim. I want to go and see her, but I'm still hesitant to leave. I guess I can admit to myself that I'm not sure if it's because of Uncle Joe being sick or if it's the thought of seeing Noelle again in a room full of strangers. My heart skips a beat thinking about her smile.

"You're certainly dressed for it," he grins, mischievously. "Actually, maybe you should dress up a little more," he teases. I chuckle and shake my head in amusement, knowing exactly what he's thinking. Even when he's lying in bed recuperating, he's getting into trouble. I'm not saying a word about what I'm actually thinking, or he'll be calling Noelle to set up a date for us. I definitely don't need my uncle trying to arrange a date for me. I can find my own dates just fine. Besides, shouldn't Uncle Joe be my focus right now? Not a beautiful and intelligent woman I feel drawn to.

"Have fun," he urges, pulling me out of my thoughts. He waves me out of his room, intent on getting rid of me.

"Aunt Viv will be in, in a few minutes," I remind him, ignoring his comment. He sighs and I force myself to take a step towards the door, knowing it's time to go. "Goodnight, Uncle Joe," I state. I pull the door shut behind me, leaving him to rest. I glance down at my clothes, hoping this is okay for tonight. I'm wearing dark, blue jeans, a light denim blue colored polo shirt, with a navy-blue collar and pocket. I don't really know what to wear to an art store opening and I didn't want to overdo it. Maybe I shouldn't go. I sigh and saunter down the short hallway.

I suddenly inhale the scent of something sweet and I let my nose lead the way. I stroll into the kitchen and instantly spot a white Christmas platter full of chocolate chip cookies, causing a grin to tug at my lips. "Mm," I murmur and lick my lips. "The cookies are done," I mumble to myself.

As I get closer, I notice a sink full of stainless-steel pots from dinner, as well as some dirty dishes from baking, making me grimace. They both have enough to worry about and shouldn't have to even think about doing the dishes. I grab the dish soap from under the sink, along with a sponge and turn on the water, immediately getting to work on washing them. I can't help but wonder if I'm really just trying to help, or maybe I'm procrastinating walking out the door and going to Noelle's opening. Then again, maybe it's both. I press my lips tightly together, refusing to think too much on it and focus on scrubbing the pot in my hands instead.

I hear quiet footsteps approaching, as I finish rinsing the soap off the last pot. "Tyler!" Aunt Viv exclaims, obviously surprised to find me still here. She enters the kitchen, while I dry the pot in my hands. I set it down on the side of the sink before turning around to face her. Although her dark brown, wavy hair is still styled perfectly, falling just above her shoulders, she's all ready for bed, dressed in her red and green flannel pajamas. "I thought you were going out tonight," she prompts, arching her eyebrows in question.

I nod my head in confirmation and murmur, "Yeah, I was." I pause and gesture towards the dishes I just finished cleaning. "I just wanted to get these pots done for you, first," I inform her.

"I told you I could handle it," she claims.

I nod my head and remind her, "Yeah, but you have your hands full with Uncle Joe. I wanted to help," I emphasize. I feel like no matter how much I do, I can never do enough for them. They have always gone out of their way for me. Now it's my turn to do the same for them.

Her golden brown eyes turn soft as she peers up at me, with what feels like the love of a mother. Then again, she's been so much more than an aunt to me for such a long time. "You've helped enough today, Sweetheart," she emphasizes. "Your uncle is asleep and I'm about to head up there myself," she enlightens me.

"You sure?" I probe, still uncertain about going out.

She leans her back up against the counter, directly across from me and clasps her hands in front of her. She looks up and assesses me, her eyes suddenly full of concern. "What's the matter, honey? Don't you want to go to the party?" she prompts.

"I don't know," I mumble. I plant my hands behind me and lift myself up onto the counter. "I feel like Noelle invited me because she felt bad for me, you know?" I prod. I barely hold back my wince, wondering if I really feel that way, or maybe that's just another excuse I'm telling myself to stay here tonight, instead.

She shakes her head and waves off my concern as if it's no big deal. "Don't be silly. Noelle is such a nice girl," she proclaims. "Plus, she's our business neighbor. You should be there to support her," she contends.

I know she's right, but I don't know if I should be getting close to anyone with so much on my mind and on my plate. Plus, after meeting Noelle, she seems like the type of woman I'm going to want to get to know a lot better. She seems like the kind of woman I could fall in love with. I shrug my shoulders in response instead and murmur, "I guess."

She grimaces at my reply, her eyes narrowing on me. "I can tell something is on your mind," she claims. She pauses, assessing me and then inquires, "Do you regret coming up here?"

My eyes widen in shock, and I immediately shake my head in denial. "No, of course not," I declare, vehemently. "Aunt Viv, I'd do anything for you and Uncle Joe," I confess, honestly. I would've found a way to be here for them, no matter what.

She pushes off the counter and slowly closes the distance between us, as if she's using the time to think more about what she wants to say. She puts a comforting hand on my forearm and steps closer to me. "I know you would," she proclaims sincerely.

"And I love it here," I accentuate, truthfully. "I really do. It's just a big adjustment from living in a big city, you know?" I murmur, in attempt to explain. I'm used to spending a lot of time here, but not necessarily living here full time.

She nods her head in agreement and the corners of her mouth twitch up in amusement. "Oh, I do indeed," she claims.

Her comment has my thoughts instantly flashing back to memories of when I used to come up here with my dad. We used to have so much fun together playing games, fishing and swimming in the summer and spending quiet holidays in this house. "Your father loved coming up here because it was so different," she enlightens me, her

69

thoughts aligning with mine. My heart clenches tightly just thinking about him, and I reach up, rubbing my chest as if it can take the ache away. I attempt to gulp down the lump in my throat before I speak, but my voice still comes out raspy. "Yeah, I know," I softly concur.

I heave a heavy sigh and Aunt Viv pats my hand in comfort. "We all miss him, Tyler," she whispers, hoarsely. She catches my eyes and holds my gaze, putting so many thoughts and feelings into just one look.

I wince and tear my gaze away from hers, emotions rapidly building up inside me, like a tidal wave. "I know," I rasp, my throat suddenly dry as a bone. I sigh again and attempt to elaborate. "It's just," I pause and take a deep breath, attempting to calm the tiny pinpricks inside my chest, "being up here brings back a lot of memories. You know?" I probe, sniffling. My heart physically aches, making it hard to breathe, as a memory of my dad and me stealing some of Aunt Viv's cookies in this very kitchen flashes through my mind, overwhelming me. I take a deep breath, fighting the tears welling up in my eyes.

Aunt Viv nods in understanding and smiles sadly. "I can imagine," she proclaims, full of empathy. "But you know what your dad would want you to do instead of moping around my kitchen?" she prompts, playfully, attempting to lighten my mood.

The corners of my mouth pull up in amusement at her question. I sigh, knowing exactly what she's thinking and she's absolutely right, but it doesn't make it easy. I blink back my tears and look her in the eyes as I concede, "Go to the grand opening party."

"You're darned right!" she exclaims, grinning.

I huff a laugh at her enthusiasm. Then, I switch directions and quietly admit a smaller concern, "I feel like I stick out like a sore thumb. I'm so different from everyone up here."

"Don't be silly," she asserts, waving her hand in front of her face, as if my comment is ridiculous. "You fit right in," she claims.

"I'm a city slicker," I declare, defiantly.

She bursts out laughing at my comment. "Tyler, we are not exactly country bumpkins," she proclaims as she catches her breath. "We're only a few hours outside of New York City," she tells me, as if I need the reminder.

I smirk and state, "You know what I mean." I shrug and try again, attempting to rationalize my thoughts, "I'm just not used to this small town life."

She momentarily purses her lips in thought. "You don't have to stay if you don't want to," she reiterates.

I shake my head and insist, "I never said I didn't want to stay, Aunt Viv. It's just going to take some getting used to," I repeat. "That's all." I slip off the counter and lean back against it, resting my hands on the edge of the counter behind me.

She nods her head in understanding. "Fair enough," she acknowledges. "Here," she offers. She turns and grabs the platter of cookies off the counter and then hands them to me. "This should help," she suggests.

"What's this?" I question, a little confused. What do I need cookies for? I was looking forward to eating a few of these.

She grins and proudly announces, "My famous chocolate chip cookies."

I chuckle in response, knowing that's exactly how I describe them. "I can see that," I murmur. "What is it for?" I prompt, for clarification.

"Take them to the opening and give them to Noelle," she instructs. "Tell her you brought them for her," she explains, simply.

"Why?" I probe. "She told me there would be plenty of cookies there." Since she already has special desserts and drinks for the opening tonight, why would I bring my own?

Aunt Viv plants her hands on her hips and glares up at me. "Tyler Jensen," she scolds. I cringe at the use of my full name. "Have I not taught you anything?" she challenges, as if she's demanding an answer. I open my mouth to reply, but quickly snap it closed, as she continues. "She gave you cookies for Uncle Joe," she reminds me, as if I've already forgotten. "You ought to give her something back," she asserts.

"She said that she's going to have plenty of cookies and other things there," I repeat my thoughts aloud.

She grins and arches her eyebrows in challenge. "But not my famous chocolate chip cookies," she emphasizes, playfully.

I give her a crooked smile and nod in agreement. "True," I mumble.

"And don't you eat any unless she offers," she warns.

"Yes, Ma'am," I acknowledge, instantly.

I walk to the front closet and pull my coat off the hanger, and slip it on. "Tell her I need my dish back when she's done, okay?" she requests.

I nod my head in agreement. "Will do."

Aunt Viv steps up to me and pushes up on her tiptoes, placing a kiss on my cheek. I turn and start to walk towards the front door, when her voice halts my footsteps. "Goodnight, Ty. Love you," she declares, grinning at me.

I spin around and step back towards her. I murmur my reply with a small smile on my lips, "I love you too, Aunt Viv." She takes a step away from me and walks out of the kitchen. I pause before I call for her attention. "Hey, Aunt Vivienne?"

She stops and spins around, looking at me as she arches her eyebrows in question. "Yes?" she inquires.

"Thanks," I murmur, hoarsely.

I clear my throat as she smiles and walks up the stairs and down the hall to her bedroom and Uncle Joe. I grasp the platter of cookies and turn towards the front door. I guess I'm finally ready to go to the opening and hopefully I will have the chance and the courage to get to know Noelle better. I admit, I really hope she doesn't have a boyfriend. I gulp down the lump in my throat at the thought and make my way to my car with the platter clasped safely in my hands.

Chapter 8

Noelle

I wave goodbye to Mr. and Mrs. Samson as they walk out the front door. "Thank you so much for coming," I say the same words I've had on repeat all night. I turn around and exhale slowly, as a feeling of both relief and accomplishment wash over me. I'm thankful the night is over, but thrilled it went so well. Honestly, it turned out to be more than I could've hoped. I glance around the store, now empty except for my family. I spot Dylan sitting on one of the black leather benches, with his coat already on. He's tossing a gold, plastic ornament up and catching it, over and over again in attempt to entertain himself. I fight not to roll my eyes, as he pauses only to cover his mouth, as he yawns.

I saunter towards Jackie, mom and dad, as they exit the back room with their coats in hand. The corners of my mouth curve upward, as I overhear them talk about my work. "It's not just because I'm her dad, it's because each one is a masterpiece," he claims. My mom grins and nods in agreement. Listening to them, an overwhelming sense of pride washes over me.

They all turn their smiles on me as I approach. Dad immediately wraps me up in a tight embrace, my arms wrapping around his waist, returning his hug. "We are so proud of you," he proclaims, ardently. "I would say tonight was a successful night," he declares, with a wide smile.

"Totally," Jackie agrees, emphatically.

"Mom," Dylan calls, sounding completely exasperated. "Can we go?" he requests, impatiently. "I have my game tomorrow," he reminds us.

Mom gasps in realization. "Oh, Dylan, I'm so sorry!" she exclaims. "We've gotta' go," she reiterates, as she glances at the gold watch on her left wrist.

Dad nods at Dylan and agrees, "Yeah, you've gotta' get to bed and get some sleep for tomorrow."

"You guys go ahead," I encourage them. "I'll be home in a few," I inform them. I just want to take one last look around and make sure everything is cleaned up and put away in the right place before I head home.

Mom wraps her arms around me and I return her embrace. She gives me an extra light squeeze and proclaims, "I am so proud of you, honey."

She releases me and takes a step back. Dad leans down and gives me a kiss on my forehead. "So am I," he reiterates.

"I'm proud of you too," Dylan utters. Then he turns and walks out the door, attempting to avoid everyone's gaze.

I bite my lip, trying to hide my surprise. That's high praise coming from my little brother. "Thank you," I murmur.

"Bedtime," Dad repeats and follows him out.

"Goodnight," Mom calls and swiftly chases after them.

Jackie stops in front of me, ready to help with whatever I need, but she looks exhausted. "Jackie, you go ahead," I insist. She's already done so much to help.

"Are you sure?" she probes.

I nod in confirmation. "Absolutely. You've done more than enough tonight." I honestly don't think I could have done it without her. "Thank you."

"Okay," she reluctantly agrees. She leans towards me, giving me a hug as my arms wrap around her back, squeezing her tightly in appreciation. "I'll see you at home," she states. She releases me and mumbles, "Bye, Noelle." She takes a step towards the door and pauses, looking back at me. "I'm so proud of you," she states, reiterating the same sentiments I just heard from the rest of our family, but I'm incredibly grateful every single time.

My chest clenches, overwhelmed with emotion as I wave goodbye. I can't stop the smile that covers my face as I watch her walk out the door. Then, I turn around and stride towards the back of the store to begin cleaning up.

Only a few minutes have passed when I hear the front door swing open, causing me to realize I forgot to lock it again. I stop in my tracks and spin around, opening my mouth to let the person know we're closed. I gasp, my breath catching in my throat at the sight of Tyler standing in the doorway. He looks incredibly handsome in dark, fitted jeans, a blue, collared shirt and his black, quilted winter coat.

"Hey, Noelle," he greets me, with a heart-melting smile.

I grin and clear my throat, happy to see him. "Hey, Tyler," I reply. His green eyes sparkle as I slowly close the distance between us.

He lets his eyes quickly roam my shop and then almost instantly returns his gaze to me. "It's over?" he questions.

"Yeah," I confirm, nodding my head in confirmation. "You missed it," I announce.

"You're kidding," he mumbles. He releases a heavy breath, sounding disappointed.

"Nope," I confirm, popping the p. "It's after ten," I state.

He winces and instantly apologizes, "I'm sorry. I got caught up helping Aunt Viv cleanup after dinner and getting

Uncle Joe to bed. I lost track of time," he explains, regretfully.

"It's okay," I appease him. Although, I would have loved it if he were able to make it, we did just meet today and he's here now. I'm just really happy he came at all. "Really, it's alright," I reiterate.

My gaze drifts down to what he's holding in front of him, and I freeze. It feels as if my heart stutters and I struggle to take a breath. I gulp and force myself to take a slow breath in and then out, but I can't take my eyes off what he has in his hands. He's holding a large platter with green Christmas holly, accented with red berries, painted around the edge of the plate and it's filled with chocolate chip cookies. It appears to be nearly the exact same thing I just painted earlier today, as if I used the plate in front of me to create the painting, but that's impossible. The cookies even seem to be stacked the same way on the platter. I don't understand.

Tyler's eyebrows draw down in concern. "Are you okay?" he prompts gently.

I nod my head feeling a little dizzy. I gulp down the lump in my throat and mumble, "Yeah." I rub my hands nervously together and force myself to lift my head, meeting his eyes. I'm not quite sure what to say and I quickly toss out a lame excuse, "I'm just tired." Although, I'm completely exhausted, that's not what suddenly has me so anxious.

He nods his head in understanding and lifts the plate a little bit higher, bringing my attention right back to it. "Here," he offers. "I brought these for you," he announces, sweetly.

My stomach twists as my eyebrows draw down in bewilderment. There has to be some kind of explanation. "Thank you," I mumble.

"You're welcome," he replies, grinning. I uneasily look back at the platter of cookies, perplexed and nervous. How do I even react to this? "Can I drive you home?" he offers.

"Ah, Um, I...I live around the block," I stammer.

"Then I'll walk you home," he suggests.

I shake my head still staring at the plate of cookies, apprehensively. "No, I can walk on my own," I assert.

"I'm not going to let you walk home by yourself late at night," he declares. "Plus, you can tell me all about this opening that I missed tonight," he proposes, appearing hopeful. I return my eyes to his, meeting his gaze and my heart briefly lodges itself in my throat.

I nod my head and gulp down the lump in my throat. "Yeah, alright," I rasp, awkwardly. "If you insist," I finally agree, pasting a smile on my face.

I step past him and stride for the front door with mock confidence. He arches his eyebrows in question. Confused, he prompts, "Are you locking us in?"

I turn the lock and spin on me heel, marching back towards him. "Yes," I confirm. "The last time I left my door unlocked, some man walked in," I remind him.

"You mean Santa," he prods, arching his eyebrow in challenge. "From this afternoon?" he adds, for clarification, the corners of his lips quirking up in amusement.

I giggle softly, feeling my face heat in embarrassment at the absurdity of this conversation. "Right. Santa," I concur, sarcastically. I pause and glance uneasily from him to the plate and back to him, feeling like I'm at a loss as to how to explain any of this. I take a deep breath and finally blurt out a question, hoping to get some clarity, "Did Daphne tell you about the cookies?"

His eyebrows draw down, obviously confused by my inquiry. "What cookies?" he asks, perplexed.

"These cookies," I affirm, gesturing to the platter he's still holding.

He shakes his head, appearing even more puzzled than me. "No, of course not. How would she know about them?" he prods.

I heave a sigh. I pinch my lips together and look up at him, trying to decide if he's being real with me. I finally take a deep breath and square my shoulders to boost my self-confidence. I guess it will be easier to just show him what I'm talking about. "Come with me," I urge.

I trudge towards my art studio, as tingles of awareness cover my skin, with Tyler following only a few steps behind me. I pause in front of the easel, holding the painting of the cookies still drying. Tyler steps past me and peeks into the back room from the doorway, allowing his eyes to begin scanning the room. "Hey, cool back room!" he compliments.

"Yeah, it's my art studio," I murmur, softly, not turning to look at him. I rub the back of my neck, nervously and continue to stare at the painting.

"I can see that," he mumbles, nodding his head in appreciation. "I'm impressed," he praises.

"Thanks," I mumble. "So," I begin, hesitantly, "about these cookies." I'm just not able to move on to anything else, until I make sense of this. I have to know how this happened.

"Yeah? What about them?" he prods. I feel it the moment he turns towards me and notices my painting. "Whoa," he murmurs, obviously stunned.

I glance at him from underneath my long eyelashes, staring at my painting, his eyes wide with shock. I gulp down the anxiety I feel trying to claw its way up my throat. "You're kidding, right?" I question, hopeful.

"No," he answers, firmly. He shakes his head in denial and maintains, "I have never seen that painting before."

My stomach twists into knots with his response. "You didn't come here while I was gone?" I desperately probe.

"No," he insists, still shaking his head. "I told you, I was at my aunt and uncle's house," he reminds me.

I grimace, remembering him telling me exactly that. I guess I was hoping there might be more to it. I take a deep breath and ask one more time, eager for verification. "Seriously?"

"I have never seen this painting before," he repeats. "I promise," he emphasizes.

"Maybe I saw the plate then," I mumble, even though I know that's not the case. I bite my lower lip, nervously as I stare at the painting. That could be the only other explanation. Maybe I just forgot. Nothing else makes any sense to me.

"Maybe," Tyler concedes. "It's my aunt's," he enlightens me. "Which reminds me, I'll need it back when you're done."

I nod in agreement and reply, "Yeah, of course." I look back and forth between the painting and the plate of cookies, again, searching for differences of any kind, but I find none. Even the arrangement of the cookies appears the same. I just don't understand how this could happen.

"Are you okay?" Tyler prods.

I glance at him, and my heart skips a beat at the concern reflected in his eyes. I nod my head in agreement. "Yeah," I confirm, my voice coming out hoarse. I slowly exhale, and shrug my shoulders, not comprehending how this happened. "I'm just a little freaked out to be honest," I admit.

He nods his head in understanding. Then he claims, "It's just a coincidence," attempting to calm me down.

I look up at him and force a smile, as I finally agree, albeit reluctantly. "Yeah, I'm sure you're right," I reply.

"Come on," Tyler encourages. "Let me take you home," he offers, again.

I slowly turn towards him and nod in agreement. "Okay," I murmur. I think it would be good for me to get out of here. I reach out and finally take the cookies from him, my fingers lightly brushing his in the exchange, sending goosebumps up my arms. I gasp involuntarily, feeling my face heat in embarrassment from my reaction. "Let me just put these away and grab my coat," I suggest, pasting a smile on my face.

"Okay," he concurs.

"Would you like one?" I offer, holding the platter out for him.

His eyes sparkle and he nods his head, smiling appreciatively. "Yes," he declares. He reaches for a cookie and states, "Thank you."

I grin in response before I spin around and walk into my art studio. I place the platter down on the small table in the corner and quickly wrap them with plastic wrap to make sure they stay fresh. They do look good. Then, I grab my olive-green winter coat off the hook against the back wall. It's layered with a soft, white, wool lining to keep me warm. I switch off the lights and then slip on my jacket, leaving it hanging open. I follow behind Tyler and slip out the back door, letting it bang closed behind us. I take a deep breath of the cool winter air and exhale slowly. I glance at his profile, admiring his chiseled jaw. I smile to myself and remind myself to stay in the moment. I need to attempt to forget about the painting and the cookies. Instead, I should put my focus on more important things, like how wonderful tonight's opening went, or my upcoming projects, or talking to Tyler and getting to know him while he's right here by my side. He already makes my heart race, after only knowing him for less than a day, but I barely know anything about him. Right now, it's time to change that and enjoy my time with him while he walks me home.

Chapter 9

Tyler

I zip up my coat and run my hand through my wavy hair as we step out into the cold. I must admit, seeing Noelle's painting really shook me. The elements in her painting were incredible. It was almost as if the plate of cookies were sitting right in front of her, while she created it. I may not have said anything to her because she was obviously distraught enough on her own without me adding to it, but it really blew my mind. She had the plate detailed perfectly. Even the way the cookies were stacked appeared to be the same and yet Aunt Viv and I just stacked them right before I left. It's surreal.

I take a deep breath and exhale slowly, glancing at Noelle out of the corner of my eyes. I can't help but notice the tension in her shoulders and what might be fear in her eyes. I'm not exactly sure what I'm seeing in her expression, I don't know her well enough to be sure, but whatever it might be, I'm not about to let a painting of cookies hold us back from getting to know each other. I don't want her to worry anymore and it's obvious that's exactly what will happen if I say another word about it. I'd rather spend the time walking her home talking about her or even telling her a little about myself. Hopefully, I can help distract her from her concerns.

As we stroll out of the alleyway and walk past other stores and restaurants on our way through town, I glance around at the quiet streets. It's extremely noticeable how very few people are milling about, surprising me. I turn back to her and prompt, "Is it normally this quiet around here on a Friday night?"

She looks around, as if just seeing her surroundings for the first time, before returning her attention to me. "No," she replies, with a light shake of her head. "It's usually really busy and loud with lots of out-of-towners that go to the ski resort," she informs me.

I nod in understanding, as realization hits me. "Right. I can see why this no snow issue is causing Uncle Joe so much stress," I murmur, putting the pieces together.

She grimaces and gives me a look filled with empathy, causing my stomach to churn. "How is he feeling, anyway?" she inquires.

"Much better," I confirm, giving her a reassuring smile. "Thanks," I add, appreciating her inquiry. I pause, as I attempt to think of ways to help Uncle Joe and the rest of the town. "Can't the resort make it's own snow?" I prod.

Noelle shakes her head and smiles sadly. "No. It's just not cold enough to stick," she explains, enlightening me.

I wince and mumble, "Yikes. That must be horrible for the town."

She nods in agreement. "Yeah, it's been eerily quiet lately," she concedes.

"So why open a store now?" I ask, curiously. It must be even more difficult than normal from what she's telling me about the snow and lack of visitor traffic.

She pinches her lips together briefly in thought, before answering, causing me to smile at her splendor. She seems to have a sort of light about her, enhancing her beauty with every move she makes. "Stores are closing left and right. There are a lot of empty storefronts, and I found the rent to be really affordable. I thought it was the perfect time for me to take a chance," she admits courageously as well as a bit defiant.

I smile, giving her a look of admiration. Her intelligence and courage to take a chance on herself is inspiring. Seeing her strength and determination only makes her more attractive to me and she's already stunning. "That's really brave of you," I tell her, honestly.

She laughs, the twinkling sound sending chills throughout my body. I grin, instantly recognizing she sounds a little more nervous than anything else, giving me a little bit of comfort knowing I'm not the only one. "I don't know if it was brave or crazy," she claims. Then, she shrugs her shoulders and concedes, "Maybe it's a little bit of both."

I chuckle as we turn the corner and approach my car, sitting in the gravel parking lot. "This is my car," I enlighten her, gesturing to the white sedan on our left. "Come on," I encourage her. "I'll drive you home," I offer.

The corners of her lips twitch up in amusement. "That's silly," she replies, leaving me confused. "I live less than a five-minute walk from here," she advises.

"Then we'll walk," I declare. I'll take every minute I can get with her.

She tilts her head adorably to the side, warming my insides to my core. "Are you sure?" she questions.

"Yeah," I confirm, smiling broadly. I have no doubt I want to spend as much time with her as she'll allow.

She gives me a firm nod and easily relents, "Okay, then. Thank you."

"No problem," I reply, my heart speeding up with just a glance in her direction. "I want to hear more about this town," I request, "and you seem to know a lot about it," I add with a smirk.

She grins, causing my stomach to flip-flop. "Well, I was born and raised in Mount Holly," she reminds me.

"Hence the name Noelle, I imagine?" I inquire.

She shrugs noncommittally, "I guess. I'm the oldest and I was born on December second," she informs me, in explanation. She continues, "My parents wanted to name all their kids after special days near their birthdays."

"Oh?" I inquire, suddenly curious. I stop and look at her, fighting a smile as I tease, "Do you have a sister named Ivy and a brother named Nicholas?"

She laughs, giving me the reaction I was looking for and causing my stomach to twist back into knots. "Close," she admits. "My sister is Jackie, and my brother is Dylan," she announces.

My eyebrows draw down in confusion as I try to figure out the connection, but I don't get it. "Those aren't very Christmassy," I prod.

She giggles and nods in agreement, "I know. I said special days," she emphasizes, "not just Christmas." She pauses, arching her eyebrows as she waits to see if I have any more guesses.

Shrugging, I relent, "I have no idea."

She nods her head and continues her explanation, "Jackie was born the day before Halloween, so she's Jacqueline, like Jack-o-lantern."

I grin as her explanation sinks in. "Cute," I declare. "I get it. But Dylan?" I prompt, clueless. His name stumps me. I don't think I'll be able to figure out how his name is connected to a holiday without her help.

Her lips twitch up in amusement and she expands her description, giving me more information. "Well, he was born on May twenty-fourth."

I scan my brain, attempting to come up with a holiday around that date, but I can't come up with anything that makes any sense. "Something to do with Memorial Day?" I guess, puzzled. I stop again to watch her reaction.

She smirks, clearly enjoying this. "Nope," she answers, popping the p.

She looks at me, as if in challenge, but I don't have any idea. I say his name over and over in my head, hoping it will jog something in my memory, but no real luck. "Dill...pickles?" I ponder, taking a wild guess.

She laughs again and answers. "No! It's Bob Dylan's birthday," she informs me, letting me off the hook.

I chuckle softly and shake my head in amusement, knowing there's no way I would've ever guessed that. "Oh, yeah," I nod, "that was my next guess," I joke.

She bites her bottom lip and slowly releases it, making my breath catch in my throat. "What about you?" she prompts, changing the subject.

"What about me?" I reiterate, as we continue strolling towards her house, passing more store windows decorated for the holidays.

"Well, where are you from? Any siblings? Stuff like that," she replies, taking attention away from herself. She shrugs, as if her questions are no big deal, but they are to me.

"I'm from all over the place," I answer honestly, feeling like I have no real answer. "Born in Massachusetts and raised in like fifteen different states."

"Really?" she questions.

I shrug, noncommittally. "Maybe not that many. My dad was in the military, so we moved from base to base. And my mom passed away when I was ten, so it was just me and him," I answer, truthfully, feeling the familiar pang in my chest at the thought of her.

I can't help but notice the sympathy that instantly covers her face out of the corner of my eye, but the last thing I want, would be for her to feel sorry for me. "Oh, I'm so sorry," she mumbles, softly.

"Don't be," I insist. I push my shoulders back, drawing in my self-confidence. I proclaim, "It made me who I am today."

Her eyes widen, a spark of admiration flashing back at me, warming me from the inside, out. "Where is he now?" she inquires.

Again, I combat my own reaction, gulping down my emotions fighting to erupt before I'm able to reply. "He passed away two years ago," I reveal. "He's buried in Arlington in Virginia. He was a general," I enlighten her, hearing both the pride and the pain in my own voice.

"Wow. That's very impressive," she declares.

I force a smile and stuff my hands in my coat pockets, my nerves suddenly trying to wreak havoc on my insides. Taking a deep breath, I exhale slowly, attempting to relax. I finally continue talking, trying to explain how I ended up here in Mount Holly. "Aunt Viv is my dad's sister and I'm really close with her and Uncle Joe. I was working a job in DC and my company was taken over by a big corporation in October. They let three hundred people go right before Thanksgiving," I state, my lips pursing with displeasure.

"Jeez!" she interrupts. "That's terrible!" she exclaims.

I grimace and nod in agreement. "Yeah," I concur and proclaim, "I thought so too. I decided I couldn't work for a company that could do that, so I quit."

Her eyes widen in appreciation. "Good for you," she declares emphatically.

"It just happened to work out that Aunt Viv and Uncle Joe needed me, so I packed up and here I am," I conclude.

"No siblings?" she repeats.

I shake my head and mumble, "Nope. Just me." I pause, taking a moment before expanding on my answer. I want to tell her all about me, in hopes to learn everything about her, but that doesn't make it easy to do. "Aunt Viv and Uncle Joe never had kids and they have always treated me like a son."

She nods in understanding, the corners of her lips curving up as she concludes, "So you felt you had to come up to be here for them."

I give her a half smile and confirm, "Yeah, but I wanted to. Wouldn't you?" I prod, as I nudge her lightly with my elbow.

She nods her head in verification as we turn another corner into a residential neighborhood. We find most of the houses strung with beautiful Christmas decorations and lights. I can't help but take it all in as we walk. She slows her pace and I do the same, matching her stride. I'm definitely not in a hurry to get her home. "Yeah, for sure," she agrees, vehemently. "Now that I have my own shop, I want to be the kind of boss that people want to work for," she emphasizes.

"You have employees?" I ask.

She smiles, glancing away, suddenly appearing timid as her cheeks turn a beautiful shade of pink, but I don't quite believe it's from the cold. "Well, no. Not yet," she acknowledges. "But I have goals," she declares confidently, putting a bounce back in her step.

She looks back at me with a bright smile, her eyes sparkling, causing a grin to tug at my lips. I can't stop my chuckle from slipping out at her reaction. I playfully remind her, "Just make sure not to fire anyone just before a holiday and you'll be just fine."

"Never!" she asserts, giggling. "What type of work do you do anyway?" she prompts.

I open my mouth to respond, but pause, curious what she might think, since what I'm doing now is so different. I grin mischievously and challenge her. "Guess," I prompt.

"Guess? I hardly know you," she reminds me.

I grin and reply, "Yeah, but I think it'll be fun to see what you think I did for a living before becoming a coffee shop manager."

She purses her lips adorably in thought. "Well, a bunch of people were fired and you weren't," she contemplates aloud. "Vice President?" she guesses.

"No," I reply. Then I wait to hear what she'll say next.

"You can't be a cop or work for the government because there's all sorts of job protection," she surmises.

I nod and smile, admiring her deductive reasoning. "Correct," I confirm.

"Accountant?" she questions, causing me to burst out laughing.

I arch my eyebrows in challenge. "Do you really think I would be an accountant?" I prod, skeptically. I can't imagine doing nothing but running over numbers all day. It's just not my thing.

She grins, sheepishly and admits, "Maybe not." She studies me for a moment before guessing again, "Attorney."

I huff another laugh and adamantly deny, "Definitely not."

"Okay! I give up," she relents.

"Public Relations Director," I reveal.

"Oh! I should have known," she claims.

My eyebrows draw down in confusion at her confident statement. "Really? Why?" I question, truly curious.

"You're really outgoing. You seem like a people person," she explains.

I shrug like it's no big deal. "I guess. You're not?" I probe.

"Not really," she admits, scrunching up her nose with distaste. "I like working by myself in my own little bubble."

I nod in understanding, imagining that's her favorite place to be as an artist; getting lost in her own world. "Well, I appreciate being included in that bubble tonight," I proclaim sincerely. I watch her from the corner of my eye, gaging her reaction.

She blushes again and a nervous smile tugs at the corners of her mouth, but she doesn't comment. Her reaction makes my heart skip a beat and I gulp down the sudden lump in my throat. She stops in front of a white colonial home, atop a small hill, decorated beautifully for Christmas. "This is me," she announces.

I nod my head, already regretting our time tonight is coming to an end as I turn towards her and grin. "Thank you for letting me walk you home," I mumble, sincerely.

She smiles broadly, causing my heartbeat to instantly pick up its pace. "Yeah, it was nice," she admits.

"Can I see you again?" I request as I try to get my erratic heartbeat back under control.

"Considering you have a coffee shop next to me, you're going to be seeing me a lot," she teases, playfully.

I laugh at her response, but I enjoy it all the same. "You know what I mean," I claim.

She nods her head and confirms, "I do."

"Are you doing anything tomorrow?" I prod.

"Well, I've got a hockey game at noon," she begins.

My eyes widen in surprise. "The championship game for Mount Holly High?" I question, for clarification.

She nods her head, smiling back at me and affirms, "Yes! My brother plays right wing," she apprises me.

"No way! My uncle was supposed to keep score for that game, so I'm stepping in for him," I advise her.

"Oh, wow. That's great!" she exclaims. "So, then I will see you tomorrow," she concludes, but that's not enough for me. I want to do more than just run into her at a high school hockey game. I want some time with her to myself, like we've been enjoying tonight.

"Maybe we can do something after?" I push.

She grins mischievously and replies, "Maybe." I chuckle at her response. I watch her as she turns and strides up the small slope of her driveway. She spins back around and looks at me as she reaches the top of the drive, the corners of her mouth twitching up in amusement. "Let's see how many goals Mount Holly wins by tomorrow," she teases me.

My eyes widen in astonishment at her game. "Wow. Okay," I concur. Even if they lose, at least I will still know where to find her.

"Good night, Tyler," she proclaims. Then she turns and walks up the steps onto her front porch.

"Good night!" I call back to her, just before she pushes the front door open and disappears inside her house. She shuts the door behind her, prompting me to move my feet. I stuff my hands in my pockets as I turn back towards town and begin walking, not able to stop the broad smile from covering my face, but then again, I don't really want to.

Chapter 10

Noelle

I pick up my new paintbrush and add a touch of a darker blue paint to the end, dabbing it on my palette so it doesn't glob on my work. Then I lightly brush in short even strokes on the canvas to show creases in the hockey player's uniform, depicting his movements. I stand back and tap the handle of the brush against my chin as I assess my painting, trying to decide if my work is finished. The painted image is a depiction of my brother on the ice rink. He's in his red hockey jersey with a thick, blue stripe around the middle and a thin white stripe on each side of the blue as well as a white stripe outlining the V-neck. He's holding his hockey stick with his left hand, while he lowers himself to his right knee towards the ice, celebrating his goal against their local rival Waterbury. I even painted his last name and his number, number seventy-six, on the back of the jersey. The ref stands on the ice, holding his arm out as he makes the call and signals the goal. I pause and tap my paintbrush against my chin, scrutinizing the painted canvas, trying to make sure I don't miss any details. I want it to be perfect, so I can give it to Dylan as a gift for Christmas. I really hope he'll like it.

The bell rings at the front of the shop, drawing my attention away from my painting. I rinse my paintbrush in a cup of water before I set it down. Then, I quickly pull my red smock over my head and place it on the shelf next to my easel. I wipe my hands on a cloth, making sure I don't have any paint on my hands. I glance down at myself and smooth out my navy-blue shirt, accented with a large white block on the bottom right and a red block on the bottom left. I check my dark blue jeans and duck boots as well, making sure paint didn't find its way onto any of my clothes, before I quickly stride into the store to see who's here.

I smile the moment I step into the front of the shop, instantly noticing Professor Shaw. He's dressed in slate gray dress pants and a blue-gray and white striped button-down dress shirt, covered with a black wool coat and accented with a cherry red scarf, giving him a festive look. I approach him, while he stands in front of the painting of chocolate chip cookies I finished yesterday.

"Good morning, Professor Shaw!" I happily greet him.

He spins towards me with a welcoming smile, "Good morning, Noelle. How are you doing today?" he questions. He steps in front of the counter to wait for me.

"I'm great!" I exclaim. "How are you?" I prompt. I reach underneath the counter and pull out the white gift bag I had set aside early this morning and wait for his response.

"Fantastic," he proclaims. "I love this painting!" he praises me. "It wasn't here last night, was it?" he questions.

My eyes widen in surprise at his observation. I shake my head and confirm, "No, it wasn't. Last night it was still wet, so I had it in the back."

"Is it for sale?" he prods.

"Not yet," I inform him.

He nods thoughtfully and then advises, "Well, you should try selling it to the bakery or the coffee shop next door."

I smile reverently. "My mom said the same thing," I inform him.

"It's very interesting," he admires.

"Thank you," I murmur, appreciatively. I reach into the gift bag and pull out two small white jewelry boxes. I open the first, revealing the pair of earrings I made this morning for his daughter. "And, here we are," I announce, as I hold them out for him to see.

Professor Shaw gasps in admiration. "Noelle!" he exclaims. "These are perfect. They're beautiful," he insists.

"Silver, sparkly and sweet," I repeat his words, explaining the dangly star design. "Just like you asked," I add, hoping he really does like them.

"You can say that again," he states, appearing satisfied. "Molly is going to love them," he gushes. "You're very talented," he compliments.

I feel my cheeks warm with pride. "I'm so glad," I admit. I put the earrings back in the box and then replace the cover, before setting them back in the giftbag. Then I pull out a long, thin, white box. I take off the lid and hold it out to him. "And I made this for you as well," I reveal, biting the inside of my cheek in anticipation, closely watching his reaction.

His eyes widen in surprise as he admires the necklace. I made it keeping the earrings in mind, but also so it would be able to stand on its own. Like the earrings, I used silver, with three layers, each one a little longer than the last. The first and third layer are adorned with tiny silver stars and the middle layer has clear sparkly crystals, all with space in between. "I love this!" he proclaims, glancing back and forth between the necklace and me.

I blush a little deeper and divulge, "I knew you would. I made it this morning with you in mind. It's a gift," I tell him. I just wanted to do something special for him and his family. He's done so much for me over the years. After all, I don't know if I would be here opening my own shop if it weren't for him. He was such an amazing and inspiring teacher.

He tilts his head to the side and opens his mouth, presumably to argue. "Noelle," he begins.

I hold my hand out in refusal, immediately interrupting him. I firmly insist, "No, it's a gift. I wanted to do something for you to thank you for being such a wonderful teacher," I reiterate. "I thought you could share it with your wife or daughter," I suggest.

He looks slightly taken aback, before offering me a grateful smile. "Okay. A gift graciously received," he agrees. I return his smile as I put the lid back on the box and slip it into the gift bag before he has a chance to change his mind. "Come give your old professor a hug," he requests, urging me by holding his arms out towards me. I stride around the counter and step into his embrace. "You're a true delight," he praises.

I take a step back and drop my arms to my sides as I smile up at him. "It was so great seeing you, Professor Shaw," I proclaim emphatically.

"You too, Noelle," he repeats. "You should come down and visit sometime," he suggests.

I nod in agreement. "I promise, I will. Maybe this spring," I propose. When I'm able to go for a visit depends on when I can get away from the shop for a little while, but hopefully by spring I have at least one person working for me that could handle everything at The First Noelle while I'm gone.

"That would be lovely," he concurs.

I reach for the gift bag and tie a red ribbon on top in a simple bow, holding the handles together. Grabbing a pair of scissors, I run the edge over each end, curling the ends and smiling in satisfaction. "And here we go," I announce, as I hold the bag out for him.

"Again, I'm very proud of you, Noelle," he reiterates.

I feel heat flare inside my chest and my cheeks redden again, without my consent. "Thank you," I murmur.

"Congratulations," he repeats. He picks up the gift bag and grins, joyful. "Merry Christmas, Noelle!" he exclaims.

I smile and reply, "Thank you and Merry Christmas to you too! Drive safe!"

I watch as Professor Shaw walks out the front door of my shop. I wave and turn back towards the back room as the door closes behind him. I glance at the time and grimace, knowing it's time to cleanup my mess, so I can leave for Dylan's game soon. I don't want to get lost in my work again and end up being late for his game. I grab the paintbrush I was using and step across the hall, bringing it over to the bathroom sink to clean it off. I turn the faucet on, rinsing off the paint before turning the water off.

At that moment, I hear the entrance bell ringing again, alerting me to someone entering my shop. Since I'm not expecting anyone and the sign in the window still states, closed, I smile to myself, figuring Professor Shaw may have forgotten something.

I set the paintbrush on a paper towel on the windowsill to dry and stride out of the bathroom, making my way towards the front of the store. "What did you forget?" I call out as I step into the room.

I lift my head, looking up as I reach the counter and my breath catches in my throat at the sight of Tyler striding into the store. He looks really good dressed casually in worn jeans, a gray, half-zip pullover, and the same black, quilted winter coat and black sneakers as the last time I saw him. My eyes drift to the poinsettia plant he's carrying. A slow smile spreads across my face and I force myself to exhale slowly and keep moving towards him. I stop in front of him and greet him, suddenly feeling shy. "Hi," I murmur.

"Hi," he replies, grinning.

"I didn't think I was going to see you until after the game," I confess, but this is definitely a happy surprise.

He nods his head in acknowledgement. "Yeah, I know, but I just saw someone come out of your shop and I wanted to drop this off for you," he explains, holding out the poinsettia plant to me as proof.

I reach out and take the plant from him. My fingertips gently brush against his as he hands it to me making me gasp softly at the unexpected touch as butterflies erupt in my stomach. I take a deep breath and smile up at him in appreciation. "How sweet. Thank you," I mumble.

"You're welcome. I mean, I know it's not a traditional bouquet of roses, but I thought it would go with the theme of your shop," he blurts out, awkwardly.

My smile widens at his explanation, appreciating the gesture even more. "You really didn't have to do that," I claim. At the same time, I can't help but be happy he did.

He grins, his green eyes sparkling with mischief as he responds. "And you didn't have to take me under your wing," he states.

I laugh at his reply, as I spin around and set the plant down on the counter by the register. "I'm hardly taking you under my wing," I murmur.

He shrugs his shoulders, still grinning. "Well, you've been nice to me," he proclaims, "and you've shown me around a bit," he adds, shrugging his shoulders again as he watches me closely.

My eyebrows draw down in confusion, wondering what he's talking about. I shake my head in denial and mutter, "No, I haven't."

He smirks and prompts, "Would you like to?"

I feel my shoulders relax and I laugh, charmed at his approach. "I don't know, Tyler," I begin, slightly hesitant, but I'm not even sure why. I'm obviously interested in this man, but then again, I have so much on my plate with opening my new shop. Do I have time for whatever this is or what it might be?

"Look," he starts, "I'm not asking you to marry me. We can start by going to the game together," he suggests.

"Together?" I prod, slightly puzzled. "I thought you were the scorekeeper," I remind him of our earlier conversation.

He nods in confirmation. "I am, but you could introduce me to some people," he proposes. "You seem to know everyone in this town."

The corners of my lips twitch up in amusement. "Well, not everyone," I proclaim with a touch of sarcasm.

He chuckles lightly and prompts, "Are you going to make me beg?"

I giggle and my stomach begins to twist into knots. I can't seem to stop myself from teasing him, enjoying our spirited banter. "Maybe," I prod.

He clasps his hands together and does exactly that, expanding my amusement. "Please? Please will you go to the game with me?" he requests, dragging out the 'e' in please. "Pretty, pretty please? I don't have anyone to go to the game with me," he emphasizes, playfully.

"Okay, Okay!" I agree, laughing. "I was about to leave anyway," I happily concede.

He stands up straight, squares his shoulders and grins broadly, obviously satisfied with himself. "Alright, let's go," he encourages.

"Just let me shut off the lights," I request. Then I bite my lower lip to stop myself from saying anything else.

I walk into my small art studio with Tyler following behind me. I grab my navy-blue coat off the table under the window and slip it on. It's adorned with red, white and blue stripes on both cuffs and along the waistband, matching my top.

"Your latest masterpiece?" Tyler probes.

I spin around and follow his gaze, instantly realizing he's referring to the hockey painting I just finished for my brother, still sitting on the easel. "Yeah," I agree. "I don't know about masterpiece," I mumble, "but yeah. I just finished painting it," I inform him.

"It's good," he declares, confidently.

I tilt my head to the side, attempting to read his expression to see if he truly means it, or if he's just being nice. "You sure?" I prod.

He nods in confirmation, an appreciative smile on his face. "Yeah. I'd hang it on my wall," he insists.

I breathe a small sigh of relief. Hearing his opinion gives a small boost to my self-confidence. "Oh, good. I painted it for my brother," I enlighten him.

"That's him?" he questions. He points to the player on my painting, celebrating his goal on the ice.

I nod in confirmation. "Yup," I state, popping the p. "Number seventy-six," I announce, the pride obvious in my voice. He may be my little brother and annoy me often enough, but I'm also happy he's my little brother. I wouldn't want it any other way. Plus, when it comes to hockey, he really has a lot of talent, and I enjoy watching him play.

"Palmer," he reads our last name on the back of the jersey aloud.

"Yeah, that's our last name," I state.

"Of course, it is," he mumbles under his breath.

"Is yours Trivigno like Joe?" I prod.

He shakes his head in response. "No. I'm Aunt Vivienne's nephew by blood. Her brother was my dad," he reminds me of our conversation last night.

"That's right," I mumble. "So, what's your last name?" I prompt.

"Jensen," he replies. "Why?"

I shrug my shoulders and tease, "Well, it's only fair. You know my last name, I should know yours."

He grins, my heartbeat instantly stutters and then quickens its beat in response. "Okay, Miss Palmer. Are you ready to go?" he prods.

I nod in agreement. "I am indeed, Mr. Jensen," I declare.

He bends his elbow and holds his arm out for me. I smile up at him as I place my hand in the crook of his elbow. My chest tightens and my heart races with the contact. I focus on breathing in and out as we stride out of my art studio, arm in arm. I let go to quickly lock the doors and turn out the lights, my palms already feeling sweaty from my nerves. Then I return to his side, and we exit the shop together.

Chapter 11

Tyler

I follow Noelle out the back door of her shop and we continue walking arm in arm towards the parking lot. She's dressed casually for her brother's hockey game, and she looks absolutely incredible. Her silky, long, blonde hair hangs down her back with the bottom falling in loose curls. She turns to me, licking her red lips as she smiles, causing my chest to tighten in response.

"I can drive," she informs me.

My heart sinks. I came by the shop to get her, hoping we could go over to the game together. I don't want to take separate cars. I want to spend some time with her and continue getting to know her. I'm really enjoying my time with her. Plus, I thought this might be a better way to guarantee our potential date for afterwards. "I thought we were going together," I gently prod.

Her smile grows and she nods in agreement. "We are, but we can take my car," she reiterates. "That way, I can show you some cool spots around Mount Holly on the way," she proposes.

I arch my eyebrows in surprise as I feel my body relax in relief. The corners of my mouth twitch up in satisfaction. "Do we have enough time?" I prompt.

"We sure do," she nods in approval. "At least we have some time. It's all on the way. The rink really isn't that far," she insists.

"I have been here before, you know," I remind her, smirking.

"Visiting your aunt and uncle, right?" she prods.

I nod my head in confirmation. "Yeah, of course."

"Did they ever show you around town?" she asks.

I shrug my shoulders and acknowledge, "Well, I've been to the movie theater and Rooster's Café, and oh, of course the ski resort and lodge," I begin, trying to remember all the places I've been to around here.

"Those are the obvious ones," she declares.

I huff a laugh and prompt, "What do you mean?"

"Every town has a movie theater and a café," she claims, playfully.

"Not a ski resort, though," I remind her.

She nods in agreement. "True, but what about the special places?"

I arch my eyebrows in challenge, needing more of an explanation. "Special places?" I probe.

She grins and her cheeks turn slightly pink, enhancing her beauty. "Yeah, like the places where you get inspiration," she announces. I chuckle in response, loving how her explanation sounds exactly like the Noelle I'm getting to know, but she ignores me. "Don't tell me that you don't have any places that are special to you," she prods.

I shrug in nonchalance. "Not exactly. I guess I moved around too much," I concede. Plus, it seems she's definitely the creative one between the two of us.

Her eyes widen and she gives me a look of disbelief. "Come on. Not even in college?" she challenges.

I shake my head. "Like I said, I went to college in DC. Oh..." I begin and trail off, as the image of a place I would go in college to feel at peace flashes in my head.

"Oh?" she encourages, arching her eyebrows.

"Okay, okay, you're right," I reluctantly relent. "There is one place that comes to mind," I reveal.

She grins triumphantly and exclaims, "I told you!" She pauses, looking at me with her eyes full of curiosity, causing my stomach to flip-flop. "What is it?" she prompts.

103

I bite my lip, wondering what she'll think. Releasing it, I declare, "The steps of the Lincoln Memorial."

"Really?" she asks, obviously surprised.

"Yeah," I confirm, nodding my head. "Whenever I had a difficult exam coming up, I would bring my books to the steps of the Lincoln Memorial and study. When I needed a break, I'd just look out over the Reflection Pool and it would bring me a sense of peace and at the same time, inspire me to keep going," I confess.

She smiles up at me with a sparkle in her eyes, electrifying the blue. "Wow. That's pretty inspirational," she murmurs. "I went to DC on my eighth grade trip," she enlightens me.

"Really? That's it?" I probe.

She nods in confirmation. "Yeah. City life really isn't for me," she concedes.

I nod in understanding. "I can see why. Mount Holly is beautiful," I admit. I've always loved coming here to visit my aunt and uncle.

"Wait until you see what I have to show you," she grins, bouncing on her feet in sudden excitement.

We stop in front of a navy-blue SUV with brown and tan leather inside. "Get in," she instructs as she walks around to the driver's side and pulls the door open.

"Yes, Ma'am," I tease, grinning over at her. I stride over to the passenger side and pull the door open, sliding inside and yanking the door closed behind me, before I buckle my seatbelt. "Where are we going?" I question, already feeling invested in what she wants to share with me.

"The Pond," she states, as she pushes a button to start the car.

"What pond?" I ask, curiously.

She smiles mysteriously and taunts, her voice singsong, "You'll see."

I chuckle softly, glancing back and forth between the view outside and Noelle behind the wheel as we drive through a residential neighborhood. It only takes a few minutes before we're pulling up to a large pond, surrounded by trees and shades of brown and green grasses at all levels. She puts the car in park and pushes the button to turn it off. I notice a pathway to my right, leading down towards the water. She climbs out of the car, and I immediately follow suit, closing the door behind me as I take in the spectacular and serene view.

"Here it is," she murmurs, admiring her surroundings.

"Wow," I mumble. "This is so pretty."

"I want to have my wedding pictures taken here one day," she admits, reverently.

I tilt my head to the side, assessing the look on her face. "Really?" I prod, surprised she's revealing this to me right now. At her words, I can't help but picture her in a beautiful white dress with me standing by her side. The image causes butterflies to take flight in my stomach and my heart to thrash against my ribcage. I clear my throat and immediately shake the picture out of my head. Where did that come from? I've never let my thoughts get away from me like that, especially in that direction.

She blushes the moment she registers the depth of her confession, her cheeks turning a deep shade of red and taking my breath away. "Well, if I ever get married, I mean," she quickly blurts out, clearly flustered.

A smile lights up my face, but I tear my eyes away from hers, giving her a moment of reprieve. I look around at the pond, surrounded by tall sea grass, shorter darker green grass and several types of trees. The trees are colored both brown and green, the pine trees, maintaining much of the green in the area, while the other trees are surprisingly still hanging tight to many of their leaves, with only some spread out on the ground around them. I bet in the summer this place fills with flowers, as well, adding a lot of color. I can imagine how beautiful that would be. "I can see why," I admit, attempting to help her feel more at ease. "I'm surprised it's so green this time of year," I murmur.

"Yeah, the leaves have barely turned. It's been too warm," she concludes.

"Do you skate on the pond?" I question.

"Only when it's really cold. Dylan fell through the ice a few years ago," she enlightens me. Her face scrunches up in displeasure at the memory.

"Really?" I ask. I've heard about things like that happening all the time, but I've never seen it happen or know anyone who has. I'm glad he's okay.

"Yeah," she confirms. "It's not deep. It didn't go over his head, but he was so scared," she informs me. She pinches her lips tightly together, as if she's reliving the moment.

"I can imagine," I acknowledge, sincerely.

She glances at me and offers me an appreciative smile. "I don't think he's skated on the pond since," she adds, sadly.

"I've actually never gone ice skating," I confess, changing the subject.

Her eyes widen in shock. "Never?" she repeats. I shake my head in response. "But you know hockey?" she clarifies.

I nod in confirmation and mumble, "I do."

She grins in response and declares, "Well, you'll just have to learn."

My eyes widen and I arch my eyebrows in anticipation, giving her a hopeful look. "Maybe you can teach me?" I propose.

She grins and shrugs her shoulders. "Maybe." I chuckle to myself. She seems to love that answer. She's definitely going to keep me guessing. Well, that's if she wants me to stick around and hopefully, she will. "Come on," she encourages. She spins on her heel and takes a couple steps back towards her car.

I grimace, not able to stop the feeling of disappointment, knowing we'll have to go our separate ways at the game. I'm enjoying her company way too much to leave. "Already?" I question, without moving a muscle.

She glances at me over her shoulder and chuckles softly. "One more stop, then we'll head to the game," she updates me. "Hurry up!" she prompts, grinning. She climbs back into the driver's seat and pulls the door shut, waiting for me. I jog towards her car to catch up, quickly sliding into the passenger seat and pulling the door shut behind me.

We both buckle our seatbelts, and she pulls away leaving the pond behind. It's not long before we're driving into another neighborhood, this one familiar to me. "I know where we are," I announce. "Uncle Joe and Aunt Viv live right around here," I apprise her.

"That's right, they do," she murmurs thoughtfully. "I forgot," she admits. "So, you've probably seen Stork Landing," she concludes.

My eyebrows draw down in confusion. "Stork Landing?" I repeat as a question. "Like a bird?" I ask, not sure what she's talking about.

She laughs and answers, "No." She pauses, taking a deep breath and then explains, "It's a little area that overlooks Star Lake."

"This all looks familiar," I mumble, as I stare out the window.

"Want me to go to the rink?" she prompts.

I shake my head, not wanting our time alone to end. "No, as long as there's time, keep driving," I instruct. I run through memories as we drive, attempting to figure out why this looks so familiar.

"You got it," she agrees.

She turns into the parking lot of Stork Landing and a rush of happy memories suddenly flood my mind. She parks her car in a dirt and gravel parking lot and climbs out. I slip out of the car and close the door behind me. I look around, taking in my surroundings, and quickly get lost in thought.

I cautiously step a little closer to the edge, where you can look down at the lake and the surrounding trees. I look around and easily find the dirt and rock path, curving down towards the lake and the rocky beach down below.

"Here we are," she proudly declares. "Stork Landing."

"I knew I recognized this place," I assert.

"You've been here before?" she prods.

I nod my head in confirmation and mumble, "Yeah." I smile to myself and enlighten her, "Uncle Joe used to bring me down here to fish when I was little."

I glance back at her as she smiles reverently. "This is what I painted for my first big oil painting," she reveals, her cheeks turning slightly pink, telling me how personal the simple statement is to her.

"I recognize it," I claim, thinking back to the paintings I saw on the wall of her store. "The painting is hanging in your shop now, right?" I prompt, glancing in her direction.

She nods her head in confirmation, her eyes getting a look in them I can't quite decipher. Then she reaffirms, "It is."

"Are you going to sell it?" I ask.

She shakes her head as if the thought is painful. "Oh, no way. I love that painting," she proclaims, a small smile touching her lips.

"Then why put it in your shop?" I prod. "People might want to buy it," I remind her.

"Because I want to share the beauty of Mount Holly with people that come in from out of town," she explains.

"What if you price it really, really high so that people just think it's for sale?" I propose.

"No way," she argues. "With my luck, someone will come in from Manhattan and buy it," she states, giggling as if she's telling a joke and I'm not privy to the punchline.

I tilt my head down and arch my eyebrows in challenge. "That doesn't sound like bad luck to me," I murmur.

She sighs softly before she elaborates, "Last night I sold a painting I wasn't planning on selling."

I nod my head in understanding and prompt, "Why?" If she didn't want to sell it, then why did she change her mind?

"Because the guy that bought it proposed to his wife under the tree that I painted," she explains. "He wanted to give it to her for Christmas," she adds.

I shrug my shoulders and proclaim, "Well, that sounds like a really good reason to sell it."

"But what if someone buys a painting that I love, just to hang it in their bathroom?" she inquires, with a slight shudder.

I chuckle in response, although I understand what she's saying. Then attempting to hide my amusement, I glance at her out of the corner of my eye to assess her reaction as I ask, "Like putting the painting of cookies in the bathroom at Cuppa' Joe?"

Her brow furrows and she scolds me. "Tyler! That's not even funny," she reprimands, making me laugh a little harder.

I look at her, wanting to see into her thoughts, but I have to settle for asking, "Why do you care what people do with your paintings?"

She pinches her lips tightly together in thought and shrugs her shoulders as if not sure how to express her feelings. She takes a deep breath and exhales slowly, taking her time to gather her thoughts. She heaves a sigh and murmurs, "I don't know." She pauses and attempts to answer honestly, allowing me to see a little more inside her heart and warming mine. "Maybe because they're a part of me and I want to make sure they're taken care of."

My heart skips a beat and I smile down at her, a little bit in awe with how open and vulnerable she looks standing in front of me expressing her deepest thoughts. She blushes and bites her bottom lip as she looks up at me, appearing slightly flustered. I'm really glad I decided to stop in her shop this morning. If I didn't, I wouldn't be where I am right now and have this opportunity to see so far inside her heart and soul and I really like what I see. She's smart, driven and incredibly beautiful inside and out. "What?" she finally asks, blushing, as she begins to fidget under my intense gaze.

I smile, attempting to ease her concerns. "That's really sweet," I assert.

Her cheeks turn a deeper shade of pink. She anxiously looks away from me, as my own smile grows. "Let's go," she prompts. "We have just enough time to get to the game," she announces, redirecting my attention. She turns back towards the parking lot, keeping her eyes on her destination, as she quickly strides for her car. I watch her go as my chest clenches tightly. I take a deep breath and force myself to follow. I jog to catch up to her, thankful for her

110

impromptu tour that unexpectedly showed me so much more than just a few sights of this magical town.

In a matter of minutes, she parks the car in front of the hockey rink. We step out of the car and walk side by side towards the enclosed rink, covered with a massive white dome. I stuff my hands inside my coat pockets and voice my appreciation, hopefully without scaring her off, "Thank you for taking me around town."

"You're welcome," she replies, appearing a little more relaxed than only a few moments ago. "Believe it or not, there's still a lot more to see in our little town."

"Maybe you would be willing to show me more?" I request, hoping for more time with her.

The corners of her mouth twitch up and her blue eyes sparkle mischievously. "Maybe," she replies, giving me the same answer, I'm now becoming very familiar with.

"Maybe after the game," I push, grinning.

"Maybe," she repeats. "Like I said last night, Mr. Scorekeeper," she teases.

I chuckle and shake my head in amusement. "Yeah, yeah, let's see how much Mount Holly wins by," I mumble, finishing her statement.

"Exactly," she agrees, playfully.

"I'm not cheating for you," I tell her, just to be clear. "I just got here," I remind her, "and even if I didn't..." I mumble, trailing off.

She grins and giggles softly. "Who said anything about cheating?" she prods. "I wouldn't want you to," she adds.

"I don't get it," I mumble, shaking my head, but still amused.

She shrugs as if it's no big deal. "If Mount Holly loses, we don't go out," she elaborates.

I grimace, not liking that deal and immediately voice my complaint. "Hey! I don't have any control over that!" I argue.

She giggles again, the sound vibrating over my skin, giving me goosebumps. "Well, let's see what your luck looks like," she declares.

"Noelle!" I challenge.

"See you after the game," she pauses, smirking. "Maybe," she teases. She spins on her heel and rushes towards the entrance.

"Noelle!" I call after her as she marches on. "Really?" I grumble under my breath, smirking with disbelief. I shake my head in hilarity, as I follow after her. A slow grin covers my face and I remind myself, she's my ride back into town. No matter what she claims, I will be seeing her after the game, no matter the outcome.

Chapter 12

Noelle

I can't believe how intense this hockey game is turning out to be. I can't stop bouncing in my seat as the puck flies all over the ice. I guess moving around helps keep me warm too, but that's not why I can't sit still. Of course, it's always a little crazy when Dylan's team plays their local rival, Waterbury, but the game is almost over, and I still have no idea who's going to win. I glance up at the scoreboard for what feels like the hundredth time, but it still says the same thing it did a few seconds ago. The score is tied 3-3 with only twenty-eight seconds remaining in the third period. I can feel the tension rolling off everyone around me, no matter which team they're cheering for. Both teams have fans lining the bleachers. There's so many people holding an array of colorful signs and nearly everyone seems to be wearing apparel with their team's colors and logos, including a few painted faces in support of their team; Waterbury fans in blue and white, while Mount Holly supporters are in mostly red and white.

I sit down on the cold metal stands, no longer feeling the chill. I'm either too numb or too excited, or maybe it's both. My sister, Jackie sits on one side of me wearing dark blue skinny jeans, a fur-lined, pink suede coat and a thick, gray sweater with a high neck underneath. Always wanting to look stylish, she even has matching gray fingerless gloves and gray socks peeking out of her soft brown, wool-lined boots. Daphne sits on my other side wearing black jeans, a black sweater with a colorful pattern in bright pink, indigo and lime along with her short black boots.

Just like most of Dylan's hockey games, my mom and dad take the space on the bench directly behind Jackie and me. Similar to everyone else, my parents are both dressed casually in jeans, but my dad wears a simple, olive green, V-neck pullover sweater, with a white t-shirt underneath and converse sneakers, showing his support by cheering. My mom is the opposite and goes over the top in support of Dylan on the outside, almost embarrassingly so. I can't help but shake my head in amusement at what she has on. She's in a royal blue sweatshirt that states, "Hockey Mom" in bold white block lettering, a red Mount Holly hockey button pinned to her shirt, and a gray baseball hat with the same thing written on it as the sweatshirt in white with a hockey puck in place of the o in mom.

All of us keep our eyes glued to the ice in anticipation of the last shot, hoping we're the ones who get the chance to take it. Suddenly, with eight seconds remaining on the clock, Dylan intercepts a pass from Waterbury and breaks away down the ice towards the goal, kicking up the ice behind him. I jump to my feet in excitement, along with the rest of the crowd, while yells and cheers erupt from all around us. I scream as loud as I can, "Come on, Dylan!"

Dad shouts, "Let's go!" his deep voice carrying across the ice.

Dylan slides to a stop in front of the goal, spraying ice towards the goalie and then takes his shot. I gasp, my whole body tensing from adrenaline. The Waterbury goalie reaches out with his glove, blocking the shot just in time. I both feel and hear the collective sigh of disappointment from us and relief from Waterbury. Almost instantly after the save, the buzzer sounds, echoing throughout the arena, signaling the end of the third period and regular time.

Daphne leans in towards me and asks, "So now what happens, since it's tied?" She comes to games with us regularly, but it's not often the game ends in a tie.

"Shoot out," mom, dad, Jackie and myself all answer her at the same time.

"Oh! That sounds exciting," she declares.

"Oh, it is," dad mumbles in agreement. He leans down between us and explains to Daphne how it works. "Three players from each team take a penalty shot. The team that has the most goals at the end of the shoot-out wins. Some sport, huh?" he mumbles anxiously.

Daphne nods her head in understanding and prompts, "So, is Dylan going to shoot?"

"Yes," the four of us respond together, again.

"He'll shoot last," I add, my pride clear in the sound of my voice.

"Why?" she probes, curiously.

"He's the best player," we all reply, automatically.

Daphne's eyes widen as she glances between the four of us. Then shaking her head in amusement, she sarcastically prods, "Do you always answer in stereo during hockey games?"

"No," we retort in unison.

She pinches her lips tightly together, holding back her laughter as her eyes widen even further with our answer. "Okay, then," she grumbles. She sighs as she pulls out her phone and starts scrolling through it.

I look across the ice and notice Tyler sitting at the score table, sitting next to another young guy with brown hair. It appears as if Tyler might be looking at me from across the ice, but I can't really tell from this far away. I smile and lift my hand in a small wave, just in case. He raises his hand and waves back, a moment later his smile growing even more, warming me from the inside, out. "Oh, boy," I mumble under my breath as butterflies take flight in my stomach.

Tyler

I've been sitting at this score table, struggling to focus on the game because of the perfect view I have of Noelle across the ice. I'm barely able to tear my eyes away from her. Paul nudging me several times to pull my focus back to the ice.

"Is that your girlfriend?" he finally questions. Paul has short, dark, brown hair, coffee brown eyes and day-old scruff along his jaw. He's wearing faded blue jeans, a dark brown, crewneck, long-sleeved shirt, matching boots and a black leather coat. We've mostly been talking about the game we're watching and keeping score for, but when we have the chance, we've also discussed other sports and what kinds of things there is to do around here, since, like me, he's new to town.

"No," I answer with a shake of my head. I grimace, wishing I could give a different response already. Then again, hopefully, I can change that. "Not yet," I add, in attempt to boost my own confidence.

Paul grins wide and nods his head in acknowledgement. "Nice," he voices.

I smile and chuckle, trying to focus my attention back on the game.

Noelle

Daphne stands up, immediately pulling my attention back to her. I grab her arm and gently, but firmly pull her back to her seat. "What are you doing?" I challenge.

"I need to go! I have a shih-tzu in fifteen minutes," she blurts out.

I grimace and attempt to delay her momentarily with a Waterbury player already on the ice. "You can't get up. You have to wait for him to take his shot," I explain. Daphne sighs in resignation, lowering back to the bench and we swiftly return our focus back to the ice.

One of the Waterbury players steps up to the line. I hold my breath in anticipation as he approaches the goal and prepares to take their first penalty shot. He taps the puck and slides it along the ice, quickly taking a shot. The Mount Holly goalie knocks the puck down, making a great save. I stand and cheer along with my family and several other fans, while Waterbury supporters groan in disappointment. I take a deep breath as we all anxiously await the next shot. Daphne suddenly stands and grabs her coat, seeing an opportunity to escape, between shots. "See you later! Call me and tell me who wins," she requests.

I nod my head in agreement. "Bye, Daph," I mumble, offering her a quick wave, before returning my gaze to the ice. The rest of my family all wave to Daphne, without even a glance in her direction.

We watch as one of Dylan's teammates takes the ice. Jackie leans towards me grinning as if she knows some kind of secret. The corners of her lips curve upwards as she good-humoredly prods, "So, who's the guy?"

My eyebrows draw down in confusion and I innocently question, "What guy?"

"The guy keeping score," she elaborates, not letting my reaction stop her.

I glance at Tyler and immediately meet his gaze, causing me to blush a deep shade of red and my heart to skip a beat.

Tyler

I glance over at Noelle and smile, noticing her rosy cheeks from here. That can't just be from the cold, can it? I feel Paul's eyes back on me just before he blurts out, "Hey, she has a sister?"

Tearing my gaze away from Noelle, I glance at him and prompt, "Who?"

He rolls his eyes as if I'm being ridiculous and tilts his head towards Noelle. "Your future girlfriend," he lightly taunts, smirking.

I huff a laugh and grumble, "Good one."

"No, seriously. Who's the girl sitting next to her?" he prompts, leaning closer to the glass, trying to get a better look.

I glance over again, noticing the girl sitting next to Noelle for the first time. I shrug my shoulders and admit, "I don't know. I just met her yesterday."

"You don't know if she has a sister?" he prods, perplexed.

"Well, yeah, she does," I concede. "I just don't know if that's her."

"Cool," Paul murmurs, grinning wide. "Hey, introduce me after the game, will you?" he requests.

I chuckle softly and nod in agreement, mumbling, "Yeah, sure, Paul."

"Thanks," he replies, appreciatively, smiling. Then, he glances back in her direction.

Noelle

The emphatic groans around me swiftly pull my attention back to the game and our first missed shot. I call out, "It's okay, Kenney!"

Jackie pokes me in the arm and prods, "So?"

"So what?" I ask.

"Who is he?" she pushes.

I sigh and reply, "His name is Tyler. He's Joe's nephew."

"The coffee shop guy?" she questions, surprised.

"Yeah," I confirm, nodding my head. "He's running it while Joe recovers," I enlighten her.

"Oh, wow," she mumbles.

"Yeah," I murmur, a small smile on my face.

One of the Waterbury players steps onto the ice, getting ready to take their second shot. My dad encourages our goalie, yelling, "Come on, Louie! You got this!"

"Don't let him score, Lou!" I add.

"Who's his friend?" Jackie inquires, her whole face lighting up.

I glance at her, confused, and then bring my gaze right back to the ice. "Whose friend?" I prompt.

"Tyler's," Jackie declares, as if the answer is obvious.

We both swivel our heads towards the score table to find both Tyler and the guy sitting next to him, staring over at us with broad smiles on their faces. Tyler's friend waves at Jackie and I chuckle to myself, as I notice Tyler quickly yank his hand down.

Tyler

Paul looks at me with pure disbelief in his eyes. "What did you do that for?" he questions, accusingly.

"You can't wave at her," I tell him.

"Why not?" he asks, as if I'm the one being ridiculous. Then again, maybe I am.

"You don't know her," I remind him.

"So?" he challenges.

"You need to meet her before you can wave," I argue. "Otherwise, it's…" I trail off trying to think of how to explain what I'm thinking.

"It's what?" Paul prods, expectantly.

I shrug, "I don't know. It's creepy," I finally declare.

He arches his eyebrows in challenge and prompts, "Creepy? How's it creepy?" he repeats.

"You're some strange guy waving to a girl," I poorly explain.

He crosses his arms over his chest defiantly and reminds me, "You waved."

"Right," I agree and nod in their direction, "to Noelle."

"So?" he reiterates.

"So, I know Noelle," I claim, clearly exasperated. "You have no game," I grumble.

"I do too!" he exclaims, defending himself. "You moved here two days ago, right?" he prods, asking for clarification.

I nod in confirmation. "Yeah, so?"

"I moved here to be the ski instructor at the resort a week ago and they postponed my start date until the first snow," he informs me.

I grimace and empathize with him. "Jeez, I'm sorry to hear that."

"Yeah," he agrees, "so cut me some slack," he requests.

I think about his comment for a moment and my eyebrows draw down in confusion. I prompt, "What does that have to do with the girl sitting next to Noelle?"

He shrugs his shoulders and blurts out, "I don't know, man. Sympathy points?" he suggests. I chuckle to myself and shake my head in amusement, attempting to focus back on the end of the game.

120

Noelle

The Waterbury player circles the puck. Dad cups his hands around his mouth like a megaphone and loudly yells, "Come on Louie! We need to beat these guys! You've got this, Louie! Be the Wall! Be the Wall," he repeats, emphatically.

"Steve, calm down," my mom urges, with a gentle hand to his forearm, attempting to tug him back down to the bench.

He gestures toward the game and defensively emphasizes, "It's a hockey game! If I don't express myself, I think I might be sick."

She arches her eyebrows in challenge and reiterates, "You're a little loud, honey."

My dad sighs in temporary resignation and quiets as the Waterbury player finally takes the shot. Louie drops down onto his knees to help block the shot with his legs, as he catches it in his glove. We all jump up, erupting into shouts and cheers with his save. "Woohoo! Yes! Way to go Louie!" we all shout through our applause.

Then, slowly, we all quiet down and watch as another one of Dylan's teammates takes the ice. I cup my hands around my mouth and shout, "Come on, Chris! We need a goal!"

My mom grabs my arm from behind and gently tugs me down as well. "Noelle, don't put so much pressure on him," she scolds.

I roll my eyes in response. "Pressure?" I repeat. "Ma, it's the championship," I reiterate. "He's feeling the pressure already," I remind her.

She grimaces, "I know, but it's not very ladylike to yell like that, especially when that boy has been watching you all game long."

I blush, my eyes automatically drifting over to Tyler in the scoring box. He grins back at me in response. I roll my eyes at him, trying to fight a smile as my heart thunders against my ribcage and mouth, "STOP!"

He puts his hands up innocently and arches his eyebrows in question as he mouths back to me, "What?"

I shake my head in amusement, no longer able to fight my smile as I look back at the ice.

Tyler

"Come on, Ty," Paul pleads. "She's got to be your girlfriend," he insists.

I arch my eyebrows in astonishment. "Ty?" I prompt. "Only my friends back in DC call me Ty," I inform him.

He shrugs his shoulders and reveals, "Well, I went to college in DC. That counts," he claims.

I chuckle and shake my head, letting him have this one. "Yeah, sure, man." I take a deep breath and respond to his comment, "Seriously, I met her yesterday. I'm going to take her out after the game." I pause and grimace as I recall her maybe answer. "Well, I hope to take her out after the game," I amend.

"Can I come too?" he requests, instantly excited.

I arch my eyebrows in surprise. "Bro, we just met yesterday," I emphasize, again. I don't want someone else coming with us on our first date, even if she does agree to go out with me.

"Yeah, and?" he probes.

122

I huff a humorless laugh and shake my head in disbelief as I look him firmly in the eyes. "You're not coming on my date with Noelle and me," I declare.

"Why not?" he challenges. "Ask her sister to come," he suggests. "She can't say no," he adds, sounding hopeful.

I huff a laugh and reply, "Of course she can say no."

He shakes his head in denial. "No, she can't. If she had any doubts about not going out with you, she will reconsider because her sister will be there," he reasons.

I can't help but admit he's got a point. Finally, I sigh and relent, "Yeah. Maybe."

He smirks, satisfied with my response. He leans back in his seat, suddenly full of confidence. "And you said I have no game," he grumbles under his breath.

Noelle

My dad leans down between Jackie and me, suddenly paying attention to our conversation. "What boy?" he inquires, silently demanding an answer through narrowed eyes.

I ignore his question and focus on the game. Chris approaches the goal, pulls his stick back and eagerly takes the shot. The Waterbury goalie makes the save, blocking the shot near the corner of the goal. I groan in disappointment and drop back down to the bench.

Jackie smiles flirtatiously and waves towards the score table. My eyes widen in surprise. I quickly grab her hand and pull it down. "What are you doing?" I inquire, anxiously.

She grins and her cheeks turn a darker shade of pink. "He waved to me," she murmurs.

I arch my eyebrows and challenge, "So?"

She shrugs her shoulders with a small smile lighting up her face and admits, "I'm waving back."

"Do you know him?" I ask. I narrow my eyes, glancing over at him, but I don't think I know who he is.

"No," she admits. She shrugs like it's no big deal and reminds me, "But he's sitting next to your boyfriend."

My heart skips a beat and I respond defensively, "Tyler is not my boyfriend." I take a deep breath to calm my nerves and remind her, "I just met him yesterday."

She smirks and proceeds to taunt me. "He's been staring at you the whole game," she reiterates.

Mom leans down, sticking her head between us again. Then, without looking at either of us, she adds, "He really has been staring at you the whole game, Noelle."

I blush, my embarrassment keeping me warm. "See?" Jackie pushes, a mischievous glint in her eyes.

I attempt to disregard both of them and focus on the game. "Come on, Louie!" I cheer, loudly. "Block that shot!"

"Don't ignore me, Noelle," Jackie insists.

"What do you want me to say?" I groan.

She grins, knowing I'll give in. "Say you'll introduce me to Tyler's friend."

"Tyler doesn't even have any friends," I blurt out. I instantly blush, realizing what that must sound like. I clear my throat and quickly explain what I mean. "He just moved here, and he probably just met the guy."

She shrugs her shoulders, not letting that stop her. "Okay, so introduce me to Tyler," she pleads.

"Fine," I grunt in agreement. "Can we watch the game, please?" I ask in exasperation.

Jackie grins as if she just scored the winning goal herself and turns to watch the end of the game along with me.

Tyler

Paul elbows me and I glance at him. His eyes suddenly widen with excitement as he questions, "Did you see that?"

My eyebrows draw down in confusion, already knowing he's not talking about the game. "See what?" I prod, needing him to clarify.

"She waved back at me," he announces, proudly.

My eyebrows draw down in confusion. "Noelle?" I ask for clarification.

He shakes his head, "No, her sister. Do you know her name?" he prompts.

"If it is her sister, I think it's Jackie," I inform him.

The last Waterbury player taps the puck and hurriedly takes his shot against Louie, hoping to catch him off-guard. I watch as the puck bounces off the crossbar, with a loud clang.

Paul groans and complains, "Man, why won't this game end?"

The final Mount Holly player takes the ice. I immediately notice Palmer across the back of the jersey and straighten. "Hey, that's Noelle's brother!" I broadcast.

"Oh. Stressful situation. He's got the last shot before sudden death," he declares as if I didn't already know.

Noelle

We stand and clap loudly, filled with both nerves and excitement, as we watch Dylan taking the ice for what will hopefully be the last shot of the game.

Suddenly, mom jumps up stomping on the metal stands and startling me as she screams at the top of her lungs, "Come on Dylan! Make this shot, baby! You've got this! Blow it past him!" My mouth drops open and I slowly turn towards her, along with dad and Jackie. We all stare at her, eyes wide and mouths agape in shock. I've heard her get loud before, especially when she's cheering any of us on, but this outburst tops every single one of those times put together. Plus, she did just scold both Dad and me for being too loud. She looks innocently between all of us and challenges, "What?"

I guess we'll take that as permission to be loud again. I shrug my shoulders as we all immediately jump up, stomping on the metal bleachers and yelling boisterously. "Come on Dylan!" I call.

"Rip it!" Dad screams.

"Shoot it!" Jackie shrieks.

"Put it in the net!" I shout.

"Blow it past him, Dylan, honey!" Mom cries.

The whistle blows and Dylan slowly circles the puck at center ice as he stares down the Waterbury goalie. He taps the puck with his skate and begins approaching the goal. He taps it again with his stick and again before he finally takes the shot. I hold my breath, feeling as if the puck is moving in slow motion, afraid to breathe. The puck barely slips by the goalie. An overwhelming feeling of happiness for my brother and his teammates spreads through me. I cheer and jump up and down along with all the other Mount Holly fans.

I pull out my cellphone to take a picture of my brother on the ice, right after his winning goal. Just as I snap the picture, Dylan goes down on one knee in celebration as the ref calls the goal, making me gasp in shock. I pull up the photo and look closely at it. It looks just like the painting I finished earlier today. My hands start to shake and my heart pounds as my blood begins rushing in my ears. I slowly lift my head, my wide eyes, feeling stunned. My gaze immediately seeks out Tyler's and crashes into his, causing my heart to skip a beat. I shrug my shoulders, feeling overwhelmed and bewildered, but not having any idea how that just occurred.

Tyler

"What's the matter?" Paul questions.

I shake my head feeling a little dazed, but not having any idea how to explain it. Noelle is the only one who will really understand, but I just hope she doesn't panic. "Nothing," I murmur, shaking my head.

Paul grins and immediately moves on, accepting my response. "Game's over," he happily announces.

I nod in agreement and gulp down the lump in my throat. "Yeah, I know," I mumble. "I'm glad they won," I comment.

"So…" Paul prods, dragging out the word.

I shake myself out of the fog and ask him, "So, what?"

"Are you gonna' bring me down to meet Jackie, or what?" he prompts.

I sigh heavily and remind him, "I don't even know if it's her."

He smirks and proclaims, "Only one way to find out."

"Yeah, fine," I agree, relenting. I stand up, anxious to see Noelle. Paul's face lights up and he jumps out of his seat, more than ready to follow. "Come on," I grumble.

Noelle

I watch Tyler and his friend, stepping out of the score box. I start to climb down the stands, suddenly feeling panicked.

"Where are you going?" Jackie questions, as she chases me down the bleachers.

I pause and take a deep breath, trying to calm my racing heartbeat. I quickly mumble my explanation. "I told Tyler I would meet him after the game if we won."

"I'm coming with you," Jackie announces.

I sigh in defeat, knowing I'm not getting out of this one. "Fine," I reluctantly agree. "Let's go," I instruct.

"Be home for dinner, girls," mom insists. "We're celebrating your brother's win," she announces with a proud smile.

We both nod in agreement and Jackie answers for both of us. "We wouldn't miss it," she claims.

Dad stops us before we take even one more step. "Girls," he calls. He waits until he has our full attention before he reminds us, "be careful. Huh?"

"Dad, how old are we?" Jackie challenges, heavy on the sarcasm.

He shrugs his shoulders as if that doesn't matter and grins down at both of us. "I can't help it," he comments.

We turn and make our way around the rink to the exit, both of us a little restless to meet up with Tyler and his friend.

Chapter 13

Tyler

Paul follows me out the rotating door of the hockey rink. Ironically, although chilly, it feels a lot warmer out here than it does inside the rink, and it is supposed to be winter in Vermont. At this rate, there might not be any snow at all this Christmas. We slowly walk away from the hockey rink and stop near the school along the path to the parking lot. We step to the side, out of everyone's way, to wait for Noelle. With no other main exit, we know they will have to pass by us as they leave. I sigh and lean against the brick wall behind us.

"I hope her sister is still with her when she comes out," Paul murmurs. He bounces back and forth on his feet and stuffs his hands into his coat pockets, nervously. We watch as several hockey fans of all ages stride by us, talking animatedly about the game, some happy and some full of disappointment.

"We'll find out soon enough," I remind him. I slip my hands inside my coat pockets, trying to warm them up. "They have to walk by us to leave either way," I reiterate, hoping it will help calm him down.

He nods his head and grumbles his agreement. "Yeah, I guess you're right," he states, continuing to bounce back and forth.

I can't help the smile that lights up my face the moment I see Noelle striding towards me. "Hi!" she says, cheerfully greeting both Paul and me as her and the woman who was sitting next to her in the stands, stops right in front of us. I glance at the woman and see the resemblance between her and Noelle immediately. There's absolutely no doubt in my mind this woman is her sister, especially now that I see her up close. They do look a lot alike.

I turn back to Noelle and return her greeting with a broad smile. "Hi. Great game, huh?" I prompt.

"Definitely," she happily agrees, nodding her head.

I move my attention to the woman standing next to her and smile politely. "You must be Jackie," I begin, hoping I'm right.

Her eyes widen in surprise. She turns away, giving Noelle a look, as if she's impressed with me already, before she focuses back on me. She nods her head in confirmation and proclaims, "I am."

I hold out my hand to her in greeting. "Noelle told me about you," I explain. "I'm Tyler," I mumble, introducing myself.

She shakes my hand and grins, "Nice to meet you." She almost immediately looks over at Paul as she drops my hand. "And you are?" she inquires, flirtatiously.

He takes a step towards her and smiles, hesitantly. "Paul. Hi," he mumbles, awkwardly. Then he pulls his hand out of his pocket and holds it out to Jackie.

Her smile broadens as she clasps his hand and slowly begins to shake it. Her cheeks turn a deeper shade of pink as she replies, "Hi."

He continues to shake her hand, slowly and stare at her in awe. Obviously not knowing what to say, he repeats, "Hi."

I shake my head in amusement and bring my attention back to Noelle. I'm not able to stop the look of amazement on my face as I stare down at her thinking about what just occurred. It's clear to me she has so much going for her, but I honestly have no idea how she could do something like this. I know she's talented, but how did she make her painting come true? Or maybe she painted what she hoped would happen. Is Dylan's goal celebration something she's witnessed often and today was just coincidence? After the whole thing with the cookies, though, it feels like this is so much more, almost magical. I'm not really sure, but any way I look at it, I'm completely astounded by her and what she can do. I lean my head down towards hers and whisper, "How did you do that?"

She grimaces and her eyes widen as an anxious look crosses her face. She bites her lower lip nervously and then releases it. Leaning in she quietly confesses, "I don't know."

Jackie finally drops Paul's hand and looks at her sister curiously, as she focuses on our conversation. "Do what?" she prompts.

"Nothing," Noelle blurts out, uneasily. "A painting. It's nothing," she stammers, appearing increasingly more uncomfortable.

"You're really on a painting run, hey Noelle?" Jackie prods, grinning, proudly.

She tries to hide her wince and shrugs her shoulders like it's no big deal. "Yeah, yeah, I guess," she stammers, pasting a smile on her face.

"So," Paul begins, interrupting us. "Do you all want to get something to eat?" he suggests, sounding hopeful.

"Oh, we can't," Noelle answers for the two of them. My heart sinks in response. I thought our plans were definite for tonight, after Mount Holly pulled out the win. "We're having a celebratory dinner for my brother," she explains. The tension immediately releases from my shoulders with her response, knowing she's not just ditching me. I wouldn't want to disappoint my family either after a win that big.

"What about drinks?" Jackie proposes. She spins towards Noelle, tapping her on the arm with wide, pleading eyes. "We can have a drink, can't we, Noelle?" she prompts, begging.

"Sure," Noelle agrees, somewhat reluctantly.

"Rooster's Café," Paul suggests and gestures towards town.

Jackie nods in agreement, grinning wide at Paul. "Yeah, sounds good," she confirms, keeping her eyes focused on him.

"I want to stop by my art studio first," Noelle murmurs, sounding distracted. She glances towards the parking lot, anxious to leave.

"I'll come with you," I quickly offer, pointing to Noelle. I'm pretty sure she wants to go check out the painting she finished earlier today, and I'd honestly like to do the same, especially after the ending of that game.

She glances at me and then nods her head in acknowledgment. "Yeah, okay," she mumbles her agreement. She looks at her sister and proposes, "We'll meet you two there, okay?"

Both Jackie and Paul grin broadly at Noelle's request. "Yeah, sure," Paul instantly agrees, attempting to act nonchalant and failing miserably. It doesn't seem like Jackie minds at all, though, causing my lips to twitch up in amusement.

"Okay," Jackie happily concurs staring back at Paul. He grins even wider at her response, obviously grateful for the alone time with her.

"See you in a few," I tell them. I begin walking side by side with Noelle towards the parking lot and easily push Paul and Jackie out of my mind.

"Are you okay?" I ask her.

She purses her lips and shrugs her shoulders, uneasily. "I'm not sure. I guess I'll be better after we get to the studio to see my painting," she concedes.

I have my doubts that will be the case, but I follow her back to her car, wanting to be there for her either way.

She slips in behind the wheel of her car and I drop into the passenger seat, pulling the door shut behind me. "It was a great game," I repeat, attempting to refocus her attention away from the painting. I hate seeing that sad look on her face. I'd do nearly anything to help her feel better. I buckle my seatbelt, hearing the click of hers at the same time.

She pushes the button to start her car, staring blankly out the windshield. "Yeah," she murmurs, absentmindedly. She backs out of the parking spot and pulls out of the lot.

"Dylan's shot was absolutely amazing. He's really a great player," I compliment as she pulls out onto the road. I know today's game won't be something anyone in this town will forget anytime soon, especially Noelle. I just wish I could help her calm down. My distractions don't seem to be working.

She nods in agreement and mumbles, "Yeah, he is." I exhale slowly and stare out the window, watching the buildings and trees fly by and allowing her time to collect her thoughts. On the rest of the short drive to her studio, we sit in comfortable silence.

She parks her car in the back, behind all the shops. She climbs out of her car and quickly strides for the back door, not even looking behind her to see if I'm following. I swiftly speed up my pace, jogging to catch up to her. She unlocks the studio door, and we step into the back of the shop. She turns to the right and walks right into her art studio. She flips on the lights and stops in front of the hockey painting and stares at it appearing slightly pale. I step up next to her, trying to assess her painting. My eyes widen with awe at seeing it again. Her talent shines through in this painting in so many different ways. I repeat my earlier question, not able to stop myself, "How did you do that?"

She shakes her head, looking a little lost and confused. I watch as her Adam's apple bobs up and down as she gulps down the lump in her throat. Then, with a shaky voice she gives me the same answer as before, "I don't know." She pulls out her phone and scrolls through, until she finds the photo she took at the hockey game. She taps on it, so it fills the screen. Then she holds her phone out near the painting. Looking at them side by side, I'm amazed all over again. It's basically the same image reflected in both the photo and the painting. It's surreal.

"I mean the ref's arm is a little different, but that's oddly similar," I mumble. "You took that at today's game?" I ask for clarification.

She nods in confirmation, looking numb as she continues to stare at the painting. "Yes, as soon as he scored the goal, I snapped the picture." she explains.

We both look back and forth between the painting and the photograph from the game today, attempting to find any differences. Besides the ref's arm, I just don't see any. "Are you psychic?" I finally probe.

She grimaces and huffs a humorless laugh. She shakes her head and immediately denies, "No, of course not." She pauses, taking a deep breath. Then, she glances at me out of the corner of her eye before she hesitantly admits, "I don't think so."

How could she not be? I've never seen anything like this happen before. I can't help but ponder what else it could be? "You have to be something," I mumble under my breath.

"Why?" she questions, defensively.

I wince at her tone. The last thing I want to do is offend her, but I'm struggling to think of something else that makes sense. "Look at the cookies you painted last night," I remind her. "How did you know I was going to bring those cookies on that plate?" I emphasize. I remember the way the cookies were stacked too. Even that seemed to look the same as her painting and that's not something she could've known.

"I didn't!" she declares, emphatically. "I just painted them. I wasn't really even thinking much while I was doing it. I was testing out a new paintbrush and got lost in my work," she elaborates, sounding completely flustered.

Her eyes suddenly widen to the size of saucers, and she gasps in realization. She runs out the door and rushes over to the sink in the bathroom across the hall. My eyebrows draw down in bewilderment, not sure what she's doing or what she's thinking. "What's wrong?" I prompt.

"The paintbrush!" she exclaims, emphatically.

I feel even more puzzled and prompt, "What about it?"

"Well," she begins, "It was left on the counter with a note that said, 'To Noelle, Love Santa,'" she explains.

My eyes widen and my mouth drops slightly open in surprise. "You're kidding," I challenge, as the corners of my mouth twitch upwards in amusement. Does she think Santa left her a magic paintbrush? Noelle is incredibly talented, but I guess after what I've seen, anything could be possible, even a little bit of magic from Santa.

She pinches her lips tightly together and shakes her head in response. "No. I thought it was from Daphne," she elaborates.

"Did you ask her?" I inquire.

She shakes her head in denial and informs me, "No. I honestly forgot all about it." She shrugs her shoulders as if it's no big deal.

Maybe talking to Daphne will help Noelle get the answers she's looking for. Plus, Daphne's her best friend and I'm sure she knows her better than anyone. If anyone can

135

help Noelle make sense of what's been happening, I think it might be her; even she wasn't the one who gave Noelle the paintbrush. "Let's go," I immediately encourage her.

"Where?" she prods.

"To Daphne's Doggie Palace to ask her," I announce.

"Okay," she instantly agrees. She obviously wants answers. I wish I could do more to help, but hopefully this is a step in the right direction. I must admit, my own curiosity is overwhelming, but I don't want to say anything that might add to her worries.

I hold my arm out for her to lead the way. I follow her outside and towards her friend's shop, located just across the street from both her store and my uncle's coffee shop. I really hope this helps her feel better and more confident about her painting and herself either way.

Chapter 14

Noelle

I glance up at the white neon sign Daphne purchased when she first opened her shop. "Daphne's Doggie Palace," shines brightly, through her large storefront picture window, into the darkening sky. The front door has a window on the top half, with prairie style wooden grids separating the glass. Hanging on the inside of the glass, she has a white and blue, cross-stitched, circular decoration with a white Christmas tree in the middle and around the edges in blue it wishes for, "Peace on Earth". I push the front door open and walk inside, with Tyler right on my heels.

We step up to the tall front desk with a white, tan and gray, speckled, granite countertop and long thing tiles in various shades of gray wrapping around the front of the desk. Two glass shelves sit in an alcove of the desk, centered underneath, where a fireplace might be. A wicker basket filled with pet shampoos and skin treatments sits in a small basket on one of the shelves. Right next to it, sits a stuffed monkey dressed as Santa with arms and legs great for tugging, while the bottom shelf holds toy Christmas trees, pinecones and other holiday toys for pets. She has the counter draped with gold garland, as well as decorations sitting on top, including a stuffed snowman on each end, a red Christmas lantern, a wintery log home with pine trees, two Christmas snow globes, intermixed with a basket full of dog and cat treats and a third with even more toys.

Behind her she has a screen set up to assist with keeping the animals calm. She has shared with me before that keeping the animals less distracted is the easiest way for her to groom many of them, and not being able to see what's going on outside or up front can help, especially if someone walks in unexpectedly. She has the screen decorated with the same gold garland she has on the counter along with red and green dog Christmas stockings. The dogs on the stockings stick out as if they're the head of a stuffed animal, one black and white, and the other one gray. She really likes to go all out when it comes to decorating for the holidays, especially at her shop, insisting the animals absolutely love it.

To our right sits a comfortable, brown, leather sofa and a rectangular, dark pine coffee table, covered with all kinds of magazines. Against the wall next to the couch, sits a matching end table with a coffee maker, cups and sugar packets sitting on top as well as a small white refrigerator next to the table. She wanted the area as welcoming as possible for the owners, giving them the opportunity to have a comfortable place to wait for their pet, if they wish.

While in the back she has a rack of collars and leads next to a stainless-steel table, like you'd find at a veterinarian's office. She uses it to put the dogs, cats and sometimes other unlikely animals on, while she cuts the animals' nails and hair, as well as blow-dry and brush them after their baths. She has a walk-in bath to make it easier to clean and bathe the animals, especially the larger ones, as well as gates and kennels, where she keeps all the animals safe while each of them waits for their turn or for the owner to return once they're done.

Daphne's eyes light up at the sight of Tyler and me walking through her front door. She's holding a tiny dog close to her chest gently petting her to keep her calm at our approach. The dog is probably about ten pounds with fur in various shades of tan and has small red bows in her hair. "Hey, guys!" she greets us with a wide smile. "Who won the game?" she inquires.

"We did," I enlighten her, pasting a smile on my face. "Dylan scored the winning goal," I add, proudly.

"That's great!" she proclaims, grinning. Then she freezes, as if she discerns something is off, but then again, she always seems to notice everything. She's very perceptive, especially when it comes to me. She looks back and forth between the two of us, her eyes narrowing. Her smile slowly fades away and her brow furrows with sudden concern. "Are you guys okay?" she probes.

Tyler and I both shift, uncomfortably, not quite knowing how to answer her question. How do you tell your best friend you might be a little irrational and a lot foolish? I glance at Tyler for encouragement and I'm grateful when he offers it with just a simple look. I exhale slowly, feeling a little bit of relief having him standing here next to me. His obvious support means so much more to me than just being here would do, causing me to feel slightly overwhelmed with emotion. I gulp down the sudden lump in my throat and take a deep breath, exhaling slowly as my heart stutters. I force myself to tear my gaze away from Tyler and focus my attention back on my best friend. "Daph," I begin, "did you give me a paintbrush?"

Her eyebrows draw down in confusion and she nods slowly. "Well, yeah. If memory serves me, I've given you a lot of paintbrushes," she claims. She tilts her head to the side and taps her finger against her chin, as if she's scanning through her memories. "I think the first one was in third grade," she proclaims.

"What about yesterday?" Tyler prompts, immediately interrupting her journey down memory lane.

"What?" she asks, perplexed.

"Yeah," I agree, nodding absentmindedly at Tyler's question. "Did you give me a paintbrush yesterday?" I reiterate.

"Yesterday?" she repeats. I nod my head in confirmation and watch as she shakes her head in response. "No," she states, appearing puzzled. "Was I supposed to give you a paintbrush yesterday?" she probes.

I grimace and heave a heavy sigh, feeling defeated as my heart sinks into the pit of my stomach. I shake my head and reply, "No, but there was a paintbrush with a card on the counter," I explain.

"Okay," she mumbles, drawing out the word, encouraging me to elaborate. "Well, what did the card say?" she prods when I don't immediately volunteer any more information.

I open my mouth to answer, but I can't seem to do it. I feel a little silly. I really shouldn't have assumed the paintbrush was from Daphne, but I have no idea who else it could be from. Could it really be from Santa? The thought makes my stomach churn with my anxiety, and instead of answering, I continue opening and closing my mouth like a fish as I try to get the words out.

Thankfully, Tyler notices my struggle and finally elaborates for me, while I gratefully snap my tongue-tied mouth closed. "To Noelle, Love Santa," he announces.

Her mouth drops open and her eyes widen, as she gapes at us, slightly stunned. Then, she takes a deep breath and looks back and forth between the two of us, assessing both of our reactions. I'm sure she's trying to decide if this is some kind of joke, or if we're truly serious. "Love Santa?" she repeats, needing clarification.

"Yes, Santa," I verify, finally finding my voice. I give her a firm nod of my head, my mouth remaining in a grim line. "It was right there on the counter after you left," I enlighten her.

She shakes her head and informs us, "I don't remember anything on the counter when I left, just the balloons."

I sigh heavily, not knowing what to do now. Who would just leave a gift like that for me? One that seems to have turned my world upside down. "I didn't think so," I grumble. I should've known she would've asked me about it before now if I hadn't said anything to her about it. She would want to know what I think.

"Is something wrong with the paintbrush?" Daphne probes, wanting more from either of us. She's obviously confused by our questions and demeanor, but then again, I would be too.

I flinch, not exactly sure how to respond, while Tyler shrugs in response. He glances at me before looking back at Daphne. Then, he awkwardly discloses, "No. I wouldn't say something is wrong with it."

I cringe and quietly mumble, "I wouldn't really call it a normal paintbrush either." I giggle and shake my head at our nearly unbelievable situation. How did this happen?

She sits back and crosses her arms over her chest. She glances back and forth between the two of us again, as if willing us to give her the answers she's searching for. I would if I could, but I don't really know how to answer something I don't understand myself. "Okay, now you guys are confusing me," she announces.

I groan in frustration, wondering how she's going to react when I admit to her that I think the paintbrush is magic. I can't keep something like this from her. I don't ever hide things from her, and this is something big. I tell Daphne everything, but I'm so uneasy about what she might think. I don't want her to think any differently of me because of a paintbrush, even though I know better than to think that would be a possibility. That's one of the reasons I love her so

141

much. She'd always be there for me no matter the circumstances and she would never judge me, but it still doesn't make this any easier. "You're going to think I'm crazy," I express. I scrunch my nose up with displeasure as I twist my fingers together, anxiously.

She rolls her eyes and casts me a look of doubt. "I'm never going to think you're crazy," she declares, confidently. At least that's one of us.

"It's a magic paintbrush," Tyler blurts out the words for me that I can't seem to force through my lips, no matter how hard I try.

The moment Tyler reveals the hardest part; I feel a sudden burst of courage consume me. I take a deep breath and push my shoulders back, needing to feel my own confidence flow through me. "A magic paintbrush that can paint the future," I elaborate.

She looks at me, then at Tyler, before focusing back on me. Her eyes narrow and I know she's again probably trying to decide if we're joking or not. Then, she finally bursts out laughing, breaking the silence between the three of us. We wait patiently as she gets it all out and slowly catches her breath. "Okay, now I think you're crazy," she jokes.

"She painted the plate of cookies before I even came into her shop last night," Tyler explains, attempting to defend me, giving me goosebumps.

She shrugs and grimaces like it's no big deal. "That could have just been a coincidence," she claims.

"I painted Dylan scoring the winning goal," I announce.

She shakes her head and waves her hand, brushing that idea off too. "Yeah, but Dylan is a really great hockey player," she reminds me, of something I already know. "I'm sure he's scored tons of goals," she adds emphatically.

She's right, he has scored a lot of goals, but this one feels different. He doesn't always do that celebration at the end of the goal. In fact, I think it's the first time I've ever seen him do that after scoring in a game. I know this is distinct. I can feel it. I'm just not sure how to describe it. "Daph," I begin, feeling almost desperate for her to believe me.

She puts her hand up to stop me and immediately interrupts. "Okay, how about this?" she begins. "You paint something that could never happen, and we'll see if it comes true," she suggests.

"Like what?" I question. What could I come up with to paint that would definitely not happen and might even be impossible, but not ridiculously so?

She purses her lips in thought. Daphne's eyes widen and she snaps her fingers, as an idea suddenly comes to mind. "I've got it," she proclaims. Something like Tyler proposing to you," she recommends, proudly.

"What?" both Tyler and I retort at the same time, eyes wide with shock. She has to be kidding. This is supposed to be our first date.

"Yes. Yes," she repeats, nodding her head with her confidence growing as the idea comes together in her head. "This is a great idea," she declares, emphatically. "Paint a painting of Tyler, just as he is, in this exact outfit he's wearing right now," she pauses, gesturing to his clothes, "proposing," she elaborates. Her grin grows by the second, along with her excitement.

I glance at Tyler to gage his reaction, feeling uncertain. He shrugs his shoulders and holds out his hands as if to say, it's worth a try. "I don't have a ring and I certainly wasn't planning on proposing to you on our first date," he states, attempting to comfort me. The corners of his lips tug up in amusement.

I giggle at the outrageousness of Daphne's idea. This is absurd. "See?" she prompts, gesturing towards Tyler, as if he's the answer. "This is a fantastic idea," she repeats. "If it happens," she utters, "then I'll believe the paintbrush is magic." She squares her shoulders, stands a little taller and gives me a look, daring me to argue with her.

I heave a sigh and relent, grumbling, "Fine. Come on, Tyler. I've got a painting to do." I grab his arm and gently tug him towards the door.

"Good. Go. Get to work. Bye," Daphne states. She waves us away, practically pushing us out of her shop.

"Okay, we're going!" I exclaim, laughing at her antics as we exit.

We step outside into the cool air and just before the door swings closed behind us, Daphne calls out, "Bye Tyler." He smiles and waves through the door.

We turn back towards my shop and trudge towards the back door. I can't help, but still feel a bit of reluctance to see what happens. I pull out my phone and hold it up. "I guess I better tell Jackie we're not coming," I mumble.

Tyler chuckles softly, the sound causing butterflies to take flight in my stomach. "I'm sure Paul will be all torn up over it," he murmurs, sarcastically.

I grin, knowing my sister will most likely be happy about it too. I scroll and tap on her phone number. I put the phone to my ear and the call immediately connects. Jackie instantly blurts out, "Noelle, where are you?"

I sigh heavily, already thinking about the painting. "Hey, Jackie. Something came up at the shop and we can't come," I reveal.

"Oh, okay," she replies, sounding overly cheerful. I'd probably laugh if I weren't so on edge about this magic paintbrush. "See you at home. Bye," she states, disconnecting the call without waiting for another response.

"Bye," I reply, even though I think she already hung up, but I glance at my phone anyway, verifying she ended the call. Shaking my head, I mumble to myself, "At least I know she's okay."

I continue strolling next to Tyler as we make our way to my shop. My mind has already started formulating the painting in my head, including what colors I want to start with. I don't have a lot of time, but it doesn't need to be a perfect painting. I just need it to resemble the image I'm imagining in my head this time so there can be no doubt about what it is supposed to be. I glance at Tyler out of the corner of my eye and smile to myself. Well, at least I have a very handsome model for this project. And besides, there's no way he's going to propose to me tonight, so I don't have anything to worry about. My stomach churns as my nerves take out their anxiety on my insides as the possibilities swirl around in my mind. Right? I ask myself, doubt already creeping in.

Chapter 15

Noelle

Together, we cross the street, my footsteps slowing as we get closer and closer to my shop. There's no possible way Tyler will propose to me tonight. It's not going to happen, so why am I trying to delay painting this picture? Shouldn't we just hurry up and get started, so we can get it over with? That way I'll know everything that already happened was just a coincidence and I can stop panicking about this mysterious paintbrush. Although, I admit, I am curious who left it in my shop, and this whole idea of it being magic, makes me even more anxious. I bite my lower lip nervously, as my mind runs rampant. I can't make things magically happen just by imagining it and then painting it. That's utterly impossible. Right? I heave a heavy sigh and slowly release my lower lip from my teeth, as I feel Tyler's intense gaze on me.

"Are you okay?" he prods, gently.

I force myself to look up at him and paste a smile on my face. I nod my head in confirmation and mumble, "Yeah. I'm okay. I guess it's just a lot to take in." I pause as the paintings I've already completed with my new paintbrush run through my head, followed by watching each thing or event materialize before my eyes. It's surreal. I attempt to gulp down the lump in my throat and uneasily add, "No matter what happens."

He nods in understanding. Then, he purses his lips, as if hesitating, but after everything that happened and all we shared, it feels like I've known him so much longer than a couple days and I'm honestly not sure why he would hold back. He finally opens his mouth and questions, "Do you really think the paintbrush is magic?"

I grimace as my chest immediately tightens and a lump forms in my throat. I gulp, wondering what it means if it really is a magic paintbrush? And why am I the one who has it? Who really gave it to me? Do I deserve to have that kind of power? I shrug in nonchalance, not ready to answer Tyler's question when that only brings so many of my own. I cautiously mumble, "I don't know."

"Daphne could be right," he begins. I remain quiet, not able to respond. "Right?" he prods, sounding hopeful.

"I don't know," I repeat. My stomach begins to twist into knots, sending a prickly feeling throughout my body, starting on the inside and working its way out.

"Do you think it's going to work?" he prompts, trying another approach.

I roll my eyes and look at him as if his question is coming from out of nowhere, but we both know it's completely justified. "Don't be ridiculous," I declare, attempting to brush off the same thing I keep asking myself. "And you're going to propose?" I challenge, arching my eyebrows, my voice thick with sarcasm. I shake my head in denial. "No, of course not," I retort, as if even the thought of him ever proposing is preposterous.

"Maybe not now, but," he starts and trails off.

My breath catches in my throat, and I freeze. I gulp hard and slowly spin towards him, looking at him with clear incredulity. "We just met," I emphasize. "We haven't even gone on a date yet," I remind him, as if he doesn't already know. "Not really," I grumble. It doesn't feel like tonight can count as a date, not with how everything seems to be turning out.

He grimaces, obviously not liking my comment. "Would you like to?" he questions.

"Well, um, not...not right now," I stammer, awkwardly, looking away from him.

"But you might want to, right?" he pushes, refusing to let me off easy.

I grimace, "Sure, maybe. Yeah, I guess," I blurt out. I'm flustered by his direct questions with everything going on with the paintings. It's just too much to think about right now.

"Well, you never know where a date might lead down the road," he murmurs.

I can't believe he's suggesting there could be more for us some day. I gasp, taken aback by how forward he's being. "Oh, come on! You haven't even kissed me yet," I announce, taking it to the extreme. I feel my face heat instantly in embarrassment. Why did I say that? Why didn't I just reiterate that we haven't been on a date yet? Sometimes I need to learn when to stop talking.

The corners of his lips quirk up, as if he's fighting a smile. He takes a small step towards me, staring into my eyes, holding me captive in his gaze. "Do you want me to?" he asks, breathily.

My heart feels like it's about to burst out of my chest. I huff, feeling overwhelmed and not sure how to answer him. Of course I want to kiss him, but I'm not about to admit that to him right now when everything is so crazy. I can't stop thinking about him, but I need to know what's going on with this paintbrush first. Shaking my head, I insist, "That's beside the point."

He refuses to break his hold on my gaze, causing my heart to skip a beat. He leans in slightly towards me, causing my breathing to become ragged. My heartbeat restarts and begins to race out of control. I feel myself getting lost in his eyes, but I can't look away. Just before he completely closes the distance between us, I'm finally able to shake myself out of my stupor. I place my hand on his chest, gentle, but firm and turn my head to the side at the last second. I pause, attempting to pull myself together, as I feel his warm breath on my cheek. I glance back at him out of the corner of my eye and mumble a weak excuse, "I just...I don't want you to cloud this."

He releases a sigh, laced with obvious disappointment, but he immediately obliges, taking a step back and honoring my request. "Cloud what?" he probes.

I pinch my lips tightly together and shake my head in frustration. I don't understand what's happening, but I push my feelings aside momentarily and attempt to explain to him what I'm thinking. "This, this, this experiment!" I stutter, not knowing what else to call it.

He groans in exasperation, his head falling back. "Noelle, I'm not gonna' propose to you today. Okay?" he prompts. "I promise," he declares.

I exhale slowly, feeling frustrated with my growing anxiety. Why do I feel so out of control? Is it the paintbrush? Tyler? My new business? Me? It's all more than I can handle, more than I deserve. I shake my head, refusing to listen and stride past Tyler. I unlock the door to my shop, struggling to keep my hand steady. I hope that changes when I start painting. I push the door open and step inside with Tyler following close behind me. I quickly head straight for my art studio. "I know you're not proposing," I contend. "I mean, you haven't even asked me out on a date yet," I reiterate.

"Yes, I did," he declares, confidently.

I stop and look up at him in confusion. Then, nodding, I acknowledge, "Yeah, but tonight is turning out to be more of a non-date."

He shakes his head and proclaims, "I'm not talking about tonight."

"What? What other time did you ask me out?" I ask, running through my recent memories.

He smirks adorably and claims, "Outside, just now."

I think back over our conversation from the last few minutes and shake my head in contradiction. "No you didn't," I mutter. Then again, there's a chance I missed something he said, while I was lost in my head.

"Yeah, I did," he restates. "I asked if you would like to go out on a date with me."

The corners of my mouth twitch up in amusement. I thought that was hypothetical, not him actually asking. "That's not asking me out, Tyler," I emphasize.

"Then, what about this morning?" he challenges.

"What about this morning?" I reiterate his question.

"I asked you to go to the hockey game with me," he reminds me.

"Tyler," I laugh. "We were both already going to be at the hockey game," I remind him.

"So?" he prods.

"So, you kept score for the game, and I was sitting with my family. We didn't even sit together," I remind him. It can't be a date if we weren't even sitting in the same area of the arena.

"But what about before the game?" he prompts, making me blush. I did have fun showing him around before the game on our impromptu sightseeing excursion. "And you did promise to go out with me afterwards," he smirks, playfully. "I know, I know, if," he emphasizes, "Dylan's team won," he adds, triumphantly.

"This morning I showed you a couple special places around town like a tour guide and tonight," I begin, defiantly and hold my hands out towards my paintbrush. "Like I said before, tonight has turned into more of a non-date," I proclaim.

"So let's go on a date, then," he announces.

My eyes widen in surprise. This has been such a strange conversation. First we're arguing about what qualifies as a date and what doesn't; now he asks me out by *telling* me we're going on a date? "That's how you're asking me out?" I clarify.

"Do you want me to get on my knees and ask?" he questions.

He starts to bend down and I have a quick intake of breath, as I feel panic crashing down on me. My eyes widen and my mouth drops open in shock. I swiftly grab his arm and tug him up. "No!" I screech. My heart jumps up to my throat as I struggle to catch my breath, thinking of the painting I already started creating in my mind. "Don't you even fool around like that!" I insist.

His eyes widen, as realization of what he was about to do sinks in and he nods slowly. "Oh, right," he mumbles. "Sorry."

I drop his arm and turn around, stepping through the door of my art studio. I turn on the light and reach for the hockey painting still sitting on my easel. I carefully move it to an empty shelf behind me to keep it safe, while it finishes drying. Then, I grab a new canvas and organize my paints to create the painting of Tyler. I pick up a clean palette and my *special* paintbrush. Tyler slips into the room behind me and stands just off to the side, so I can see him, observing me. "Ok, Noelle, would you like to have dinner with me tonight?" he proposes.

"I can't," I instantly reply, with a quick glance in his direction. "I have to be home for my brother's victory dinner," I repeat.

"Oh, that's right," he acknowledges. "What about after?" he prods.

"Sure," I answer. His mouth slowly curves up in a triumphant smile with my response. I try to focus on preparing my supplies. "What do you want to do?" I inquire. Then, I attempt to put my focus on the canvas in front of me, instead of thinking about our upcoming date.

"How about ice cream?" he suggests. "My Aunt Viv said the town creamery is really good," he states.

I huff a laugh and nod my head in agreement as I search for a sketching pencil. Going out for ice cream in the winter? That's my kind of date. "It is," I confirm, simply.

"So, it's a date," he declares, sounding satisfied. "Right?" he prompts. He looks me in the eyes, pushing for my confirmation.

I smile and feel my cheeks heat almost instantly. "Right" I concur. I pull a tall, gray, steel art stool to the right of my canvas. I look up at Tyler and gesture towards the seat. "Sit," I instruct. He reaches the stool in one long stride. He twists and lowers himself onto it and continues to move around, making me smirk. "Sit still," I emphasize, fighting a smile.

"I've never had someone paint me before," he mumbles, attempting to control his fidgeting.

I concentrate on the blank slate set up in front of me, glancing back and forth between Tyler and the canvas as I quickly scratch out a rough drawing. "This is just going to be a rough sketch," I enlighten him, letting him know what I'm doing.

He shrugs his shoulders in response. "I still think it's pretty cool," he admits, grinning and then quickly wipes the smile from his face.

I laugh in response, enjoying his reaction to being my muse. I playfully inform him, "Yeah, you can say that after you see it."

"Do you want me to smile?" he prods.

I shake my head, focusing on the sketch. "No," I murmur.

"What do you want me to do?" he probes.

The corners of my lips twitch up in amusement. He reminds me of a little boy, not able to sit still. I reply, "Nothing." He nods and begins looking around the small room, obviously a little uncomfortable with me continuously staring at him, but I get it. I would probably be the same way if this situation were reversed. Although, I'll admit, it's a great opportunity for me to stare at him without feeling uncomfortable. I quickly sketch a rough draft of him, just enough so I'm able to paint the image in my head without him sitting directly in front of me while I work. He turns around to look behind him making me fight another smile. "Stop moving," I demand, tickled.

He turns his head back towards me, a sheepish look covering his face as he immediately apologizes. "I'm sorry," he murmurs.

I giggle softly as he finally settles in. We both remain quiet, while I swiftly finish the sketch, maintaining my focus. I take a step back to appraise it, making sure I didn't miss any important details that I would need him to be sitting in front of me to create. I nod my head in satisfaction, believing I have everything I need. "There," I mutter under my breath.

Tyler arches his eyebrows in surprise and questions, "You're done?"

I nod in confirmation and explain, "Yeah, well, I still have to paint it."

"Can I see it?" he asks, curiously.

I grin and shake my head in refusal. "No, not until it's finished," I answer.

"How long will it take?" he prods.

I shrug my shoulders, taking a moment to think before I speak. "I think it will take me about an hour. I'm going to lock the doors and just get this done right now," I inform him. I'm incredibly driven to get this done as quickly as possible and see what happens, hoping everything has all just been a coincidence.

He places his hands on his knees and announces, "Okay, I'm going to go next door and help out for a little while, while I wait for you. I'll lock the front door and go out the back," he offers.

"Okay," I agree, offering him a grateful smile. "Thank you." He smiles in response as I begin mixing my paints, trying to get the color I want to start. "I'll come over when it's done," I inform him. I take a deep breath and dip the paintbrush into brown paint, dabbing it against the palette. I lift it up to the canvas and start painting. Tyler stands up and I feel his eyes on me momentarily, but I keep my gaze on the canvas, attempting to maintain my focus. He finally exhales slowly and mumbles, "Okay. I'll see you in a little while then."

Instead of responding, I smile, and give a slight nod in acknowledgement as I continue painting. The sooner this is done, the sooner we can get on with everything else. I'm just not sure what that all entails quite yet. As for Tyler and me, hopefully our date tomorrow night will finally happen without any magical disruptions. After all this madness, I'm really looking forward to a little bit of calm.

Chapter 16

Tyler

I stroll into the back of the coffee shop and see Mandy standing at the counter handing coffee to a customer. "Thank you," she proclaims, smiling. I watch as they smile and turn to leave. She spins on her heel, facing me and grins, "Hey, Tyler. I thought you were done for the day." She's wearing the same standard barista outfit, as always, but her current apron has stripes down the front in white, red and green, with a red ribbon tying it around her neck and waist, giving her a very festive look.

I smirk and nod my head, agreeing with her. "So did I," I retort. Her head falls back, laughing at my response. I shrug my shoulders and immediately explain why I'm back. "I just thought I'd come in and help out for a little while. Noelle is in the middle of something at her shop that she needs to finish tonight, and I need to catch up with her when she's done. Plus, we have plans later as well," I reveal, giving her more information than she needs.

"Ah, okay," she murmurs, giving me a knowing look.

I chuckle softly, but don't comment on her assumption. "Are you okay with closing up tonight?" I ask. "You were here kind of early," I add, suddenly feeling bad.

She nods in confirmation and waves me off, telling me, "I wasn't here that early and I was always planning on closing tonight." The bell rings as another customer walks in, disrupting our conversation. She turns towards the older man to greet him with a bright smile. "Hi, may I help you?" she prompts.

I make my way behind the coffee bar all decorated for Christmas to help cleanup. There's always something that needs to be done. I walk over to the sink and wash my hands before I do anything else. Then, I take everything in, assessing what still needs to be done as I begin restacking the tray of clean coffee mugs. I really like what my aunt and uncle have done with this place. The bar area has a section up against the wall where we keep our menus, register, receipts and other various items depending on the day. Right now, it's decorated for Christmas with a snowman, a mini Christmas tree, a cherry red lantern, and an angel that lights up. Then around the old window, now closed in with wood planks from when they expanded, hangs a string of large, red poinsettia flowers without the stems and white icicle lights. The same wood planks cover the front of the bar, with the top a beautiful, sealed mahogany with about an inch rounded edging of maple all the way around. We keep the countertop clear for customers, except for a few decorative steins filled with straws and silverware. The wide plank wood floors are a shade darker than the countertops, albeit appearing a bit more rugged. We have a few small, square, maple tables and chairs for customers that don't want to sit at the coffee bar, since it can get kind of hectic, especially in the mornings. The whole place feels comfortable and classic. It's not like anything in the city. It has a small town feel to me giving me a sense of comfort. I like it.

Mandy finishes up with the customer, handing him a to-go coffee and a small brown bag with cookies tucked inside. As he turns to leave, she grabs a rag and starts wiping down the bar, amazing me with her strong work ethic, once again. I know customers love seeing a friendly face when they walk in, and Mandy enjoys the interactions just as much. She's wonderful with people. I feel like that's one of the great things about living and working in a small town, the familiarity and friendliness.

"Are you sure you don't mind staying?" I question again. I know she likes the hours, but I don't want to ask too much of her either. I feel like she's always here. I know I've only been back a few days, but now that I'm working here, it seems she's here more than I am and I'm supposed to be running the place.

"No, not at all," she reaffirms. She waves her hand, quickly dismissing my apprehension. "I can really use the extra cash," she adds.

I breathe a sigh of relief. "Thank you," I mumble, gratefully. "I really appreciate it, Mandy," I emphasize. I may need to do something special for her for the holidays.

A sophisticated older woman, with short, gray hair and blue eyes enters the coffee shop, appearing anxious and upset. She looks familiar, but I've met so many people, both from when I used to visit and since I've been here to stay to help Uncle Joe and Aunt Viv. I'm honestly not sure if we've met before or not. She's wearing black dress pants, a black turtleneck sweater and a long winter coat separated into sections of cranberry, black and mustard yellow. She makes her way up to the counter, fidgeting nervously with the lapels on her coat. "May I help you?" I request, as I approach her.

She grimaces and sighs heavily, shaking her head in frustration. "I hope so," she murmurs.

Mandy steps up to us with a broad smile for the woman, obviously recognizing her. "Hi, Mrs. Halsen!" she greets her, cheerfully. Her eyebrows almost immediately draw down in concern at the expression on the woman's face. She questions, "Is everything okay?"

Mrs. Halsen heaves another heavy sigh, sounding defeated. She winces and shakes her head in response. "No, I'm afraid it isn't," she announces, her voice shaky.

"What's the matter?" Mandy prods gently.

"I was here yesterday," she begins, hesitantly. Then she pauses and pinches her lips tightly together as she looks around her, nervously.

She seems so concerned and I have the strongest urge to do what I can to ease her worries. When she still doesn't say anything else, I interrupt and inquire, "Did something happen?"

She turns towards me, as if noticing me for the first time. She narrows her eyes and tilts her head to the side in confusion. Then she abruptly prompts, "Who are you?"

I give her a small smile, knowing something isn't quite right and hoping we can fix it, but to do that, I need her to feel comfortable enough to be able to tell us what the issue is. "I'm Joe's nephew, Tyler," I tell her, introducing myself. "I'm the manager for now," I inform her, politely. "Did someone give you a problem?" I probe.

She shakes her head, instantly dismissing my concern. "No, no, nothing like that," she states. "Everyone here is wonderful." My shoulders relax slightly as a feeling of relief washes over me, but not for long since it's obvious we still need to do something to help her.

"What's wrong, Mrs. Halsen?" Mandy repeats, sweetly, bringing the woman's attention back to her and why she's here. "You seem so upset," she observes.

"I am, Amanda, dear," she concedes, with a nod of her head. "You see, I went to put on my jewelry this morning and I can't find my engagement ring," she reveals, visibly shaking.

Mandy's eyes widen in shock. "Oh, no!" she exclaims. She steps around the counter and stands right in front of Mrs. Halsen.

Mrs. Halsen flinches and shakes her head in disbelief. "I don't remember where I took it off, or if it might have fallen off and I didn't notice," she mumbles and shrugs her shoulders in puzzlement. "I've lost so much weight since Mr. Halsen passed away," she rambles, anxiously explaining her thoughts.

Mandy nods her head in agreement and reaches up to pat her gently on her arm in comfort. "You sure have," she murmurs, her voice full of compassion for Mrs. Halsen.

"I've been retracing my steps from yesterday and I can't seem to find it anywhere. I did come in here for a coffee, but it was so quickly, I doubt it's here," she continues, full of regret.

"What were you doing when you were in here?" I prompt. Maybe if we know, we might have a chance of finding it.

She pauses before responding. "Well, I came in, ordered a coffee here," she says, pointing to a spot at the front of the counter, "and I picked it up over there," she adds, gesturing towards the other end of the coffee bar.

"Were you wearing gloves?" Mandy questions. "It was cold yesterday," she reminds Mrs. Halsen.

Her eyes widen in surprise, as if she had forgotten something. "I was," she declares, a hopeful smile springing to her face and quickly falling, "but I already looked inside them."

"Were you wearing them in here?" Mandy prods.

Mrs. Halsen purses her lips briefly in thought before answering. "You know, I was, but I took them off so I could get my money out of my wallet," she enlightens us.

"I swept the floor last night before I left and there wasn't a ring in the dust pan," I inform them, regretfully.

Mrs. Halsen winces, her disappointment obvious. "Oh," she groans. "This was my last hope," she whispers, as tears well up in her eyes. "I don't know what I'm going to do without my ring," she whimpers. "It was my connection to Marty," she adds, her voice trembling with emotion.

Mandy reaches for both of Mrs. Halsen's hands and clasps them tightly. "Don't give up, Mrs. Halsen," she encourages. "Maybe it's in a vent or something," she suggests. "We'll help you look," she offers, with a quick glance in my direction.

"Really?" Mrs. Halsen asks, sounding hopeful again.

I nod in confirmation, "Absolutely."

"I'd be so grateful," Mrs. Halsen rasps. I step out from behind the end of the bar and begin searching the corners and edges of the floor, hoping we're able to find her ring for her. I wonder if maybe I missed it while I was sweeping. "It could be anywhere," she reiterates.

"Tyler," Mandy suddenly calls out. "I think I see something, but I can't reach it," she announces. I turn towards her and see her crouched over the small metal vent in the floor near our, four-foot Christmas tree lit with colorful lights.

"Where?" I probe. She points inside the vent as I approach her. "Let me try," I suggest.

I crouch down next to Mandy on the floor and try to look where she's pointing inside the vent, searching for even a small glint of something, indicating it might be there. "See it?" she prods.

"Is it my ring?" Mrs. Halsen inquires, excitedly.

"I don't know," Mandy murmurs honestly.

I reach down and pull the vent out of the floorboards to get a better view. I set it to the side, just out of the way on the floor. Then, I lay down flat on the ground so I can reach all the way into the vent. "Let me just," I mumble, as I stretch to reach whatever it is, hoping it's her ring. I finally touch the smooth, cool metal with the tips of my fingers. I stretch just a little further and I'm finally able to grasp it. It feels like it could be what she's looking for. "A-ha!" I exclaim. I pull my arm out of the vent, with a broad smile on my face and the ring in my hand. I push myself up and begin to rise, pausing briefly on my knee, as I hold it out for Mrs. Halsen. "Is this what you're looking for?" I prompt, feeling both elated for her and satisfied.

Mrs. Halsen gasps and covers her mouth in joyful surprise. Right at that moment, Noelle walks into the coffee shop through the back door. As she strides into the room, she announces, "Tyler, I finished my painting!" She holds up her painting and freezes the moment she spots me. I'm still slightly crouched, down on my knee, holding Mrs. Halsen's diamond ring out to her, as if I'm proposing. Noelle's face instantly pales. The painting begins to slip from her fingers as she drops her arms slowly towards the floor, looking stunned. I push myself the rest of the way off the floor and stand up slowly, staring at Noelle in wonder. I take in the terrified look on Noelle's face, causing my heart to skip a beat. I don't want her to stress, or run, but painting really happened. It's not exactly like either of us imagined, but it definitely happened. The picture Noelle just painted came true mere moments later.

"Yes! That's it!" Mrs. Halsen declares, with both relief and pure delight. She takes the ring from my hand and places it on her finger, snapping me out of my shock. I brush my hands off on my jeans, as I continue to stare at Noelle and hoping this doesn't make her panic.

I turn and reach for Mandy's hands and help pull her up to her feet. "Tyler are you okay," Mandy questions, glancing at me.

I look at Mandy, her eyes suddenly filled with concern for me. I shake my head and gulp over the lump in my throat. I nod my head, absentmindedly and rasp, "Yeah, I'm fine." I glance back at Noelle, not quite sure what to say to wipe that tortured look off her face and get her to smile again.

Mrs. Halsen turns around and grins at Noelle. Her mouth widens in surprise and she covers her mouth with her hand. "What a wonderful painting," she compliments, as she looks at the canvas hanging from Noelle's fingertips.

"Thank you," Noelle softly utters.

"How did you know that Tyler was going to find the ring?" Mandy inquires, sounding puzzled. I keep my focus on Noelle, waiting to see how she responds. I have to admit, I'm shocked and curious as well. Maybe she had heard about Mrs. Halsen losing her ring? There could still be some kind of explanation, but after everything that transpired in the last twenty-four hours, I know I'm fooling myself. I think maybe she really does have a touch of magic, and although it's surprising, how can I help her see it's a good thing.

Noelle's eyes suddenly widen to the size of saucers. "I...I...I gotta' go," she stammers. Then she spins on her heel and runs out the back door still clasping her painting tightly in her hand.

"Noelle!" I call, desperately after her. "Wait!" I plead.

Mrs. Halsen steps in front of me, stopping me in my tracks. "Thank you so much, young man," she emphasizes her gratitude.

I force myself to turn my gaze to Mrs. Halsen and smile down at her, as my heart sinks into the pit of my stomach, feeling completely defeated. "Of course," I mumble, distractedly, with my mind still focusing on chasing after Noelle.

"Thank you," she repeats. "You're my hero," she proclaims, her eyes gleaming with emotion. She wraps her arms tightly around me, thanking me again, with a light squeeze. I gently hug her back, my eyes pulled back to the spot Noelle just vacated. Mrs. Halsen releases me and beams proudly up at me. Then, she steps over to Mandy, wrapping her up in a tight embrace as well. "I'm so grateful to both of you," she states, sounding a little overwhelmed.

Mandy returns her smile. "We're happy to help Mrs. Halsen," she expresses, sincerely.

I barely glance over at Mandy, before redirecting my attention to the back door. "I have to run next door for a minute," I notify her.

She nods in acknowledgement, "Okay. I'll be fine," she insists.

I nod my head in response, knowing she wasn't expecting me to be here right now anyway. I immediately stride for the back door, before anything else can stop me. I need to talk to Noelle right now. The look of pure panic on her face makes my stomach twist into knots. I definitely don't want her to feel that way, but more than anything, I don't want her to push me away because of it. We've barely just met. I want the chance to get to know her, without all this noise surrounding us. I'm not about to let her pull away from me now that we're just getting started.

Chapter 17

Noelle

I put the painting of Tyler I just completed on the easel and then begin pacing, trying to comprehend what happened at Cuppa' Joe. I stop and glance at the painting again, before I force myself to tear my eyes away, as I continue pacing. I shake my head, trying to get the actual image of Tyler down on one knee, with a ring in his hand, out of my mind. How did that happen? I don't understand. When Daphne suggested I paint this picture, I knew it was something I could paint that was completely impossible. It could never happen. So, how did it come true? I hear the chime of bells on the front door, signaling someone entering the shop, but I ignore it momentarily and continue my pacing.

Tyler steps into the doorway of my art studio and braces his hands on the frame as his eyes land on me. "Noelle," he murmurs, softly exhaling my name.

I gulp over the lump in my throat and point at the painting, feeling the panic growing inside my chest, attempting to claw its way up my throat. "This isn't happening," I complain. I feel out of control and I'm not sure how to pull myself together. My breath quickens and I struggle to catch my breath.

"Noelle," Tyler repeats a little louder, attempting to pull my attention to him.

"This is not happening, Tyler!" I reiterate, shaking my head.

"How did you know?" he questions, calmly.

I halt my pacing instantly and look at him with wide eyes, surprised he would even ask. "I didn't," I declare, vehemently. "I just painted what Daphne said to paint," I insist.

He nods his head in response, maintaining his composure. "Did you call her?" he prods.

I nod my head in confirmation and mumble, "I called her as soon as I walked out of the door. She's on her way." I go back to pacing in front of the painting.

"Maybe she set it up with Mrs. Halsen," he suggests.

I take a deep breath and force myself to slow my breathing, as I contemplate his words. "Maybe," I finally concede, not believing she would do that.

Tyler looks at the painting and shakes his head in amazement. "You even got the detail of the ring right," he mumbles.

My mouth drops open as I gasp. I arch my eyebrows, looking at him in astonishment. "Seriously?" I prod.

He nods in confirmation. "Yeah," he verifies, as he stares at the painting. "It's actually a pretty good painting," he praises.

My hands start to itch with his compliment. I suddenly feel the strongest urge to get rid of any proof of me having any sort of magic ability immediately. "You can have it," I declare, shrugging like it's no big deal. Then, I swiftly reach for it and hand it to him, wanting it anywhere but here.

He takes it from me, taken a little off-guard. "I can?" he prompts, perplexed.

"Yes," I confirm. "And this one," I announce. I reach out and grab the painting of the plate of chocolate chip cookies, handing it to him.

He hesitantly takes it from me, holding it in his other hand. He gives me a quizzical look and prompts, "Are you sure?"

"And take this one," I proclaim. He stacks the first two, just as I hand him the hockey painting that I made for my brother, piling it on top of the other two. I need to get every single one of them out of my sight and out of my studio as soon as possible.

Tyler shakes his head, refusing the gift, although he holds it with the other two. "No, that's for your brother," he reminds me, even though I obviously know.

"Take them all!" I demand. I hold my hands up in the air as if being free of the paintings will make everything go back to normal.

Tyler sets all the paintings down, that I just stacked in his arms, placing them on the small table behind us. He steps in front of me and grasps me firmly by the shoulders, holding me in place, probably so I stop clearing everything out. He tilts his head down and meets my eyes, his own showing an enormous amount of empathy. "Noelle, calm down," he encourages me.

"Calm down?" I shriek.

"Yes. Calm down," he repeats, his voice soothing.

I look at him with my eyes wide and my face pale. "I'm painting the future!" I remind him. "How am I supposed to calm down?" I nearly beg for an answer.

He opens his mouth to respond and then snaps it shut. Stepping towards me, he gently pulls me into his chest as he wraps his arms around me in comfort. I breathe a sigh of relief, feeling safe in his embrace. I lean into him but keep my arms hanging loose at my sides. I hear the bells at the front door chime again, signaling someone entering the store, but I don't react. Instead, I remain frozen, wrapped up in Tyler's embrace, as if this is exactly where I'm supposed to be.

"Noelle, you aren't painting the future," he murmurs gently, as if saying it will make it true. "They're all just random coincidences."

Daphne bursts through the door of my art studio. She gasps at the sight of me in Tyler's arms. "Oh! It really came true?" she prompts, disbelief obvious in her voice.

I nod in confirmation and mumble into Tyler's chest, "Yeah."

"You proposed?" Daphne clarifies, appearing completely flabbergasted. "Why would you do that today?" she accuses.

I sigh in defeat, not yet able to repeat the story. Tyler shakes his head as he reluctantly releases me and faces Daphne. I'm extremely grateful when he's the one who opens his mouth to enlighten her. "No, I didn't propose. I found someone's ring," he explains.

"Oh. Okay," she replies as if it's no big deal.

I grimace and narrow my eyes on her. This feels like a big deal to me. Why doesn't anyone see that? "But the painting came true, Daph," I reiterate.

"Well," she stammers and shrugs her shoulders, "it could just be a coincidence."

"That's what I said," Tyler concurs.

An idea suddenly pops into my head. I reach over and grab the magic paintbrush off the shelf. I hold it out towards both of them and suggest, "One of you try."

Their eyes widen and their mouths drop slightly open in awkward surprise. "What?" Tyler questions, defensively taking a small step back.

I shrug my shoulders, nonchalantly, the same way both of them seem to be treating this situation. "Paint a picture and see if it comes true," I propose.

Daphne holds her hands up and shakes her head in refusal. "Not me," she instantly declines. "I have three golden retrievers coming in ten minutes," she advises.

I turn my gaze towards Tyler. I shove the paintbrush in his direction, feeling desperate. "Then, you try, Tyler," I plead.

"I don't know the first thing about painting," he argues, looking uncomfortable. "I don't think I've painted anything since elementary school.

I scramble to remove the painting of Tyler he just placed back on the easel, along with the two other paintings I handed him, getting all of them out of the way. "I'll help you," I insist.

He winces and looks towards the empty easel, now in front of him. "Noelle," he says my name, his uncertainty clear.

I interrupt him, before he has a chance to give me even one more reason why this is a bad idea. "Please," I beg, needing him to do this for me.

He sighs heavily in resignation, causing my heart to skip a beat, even with my attention focused elsewhere. "What do you want me to paint?" he prompts, sounding exhausted.

I shrug my shoulders and suggest, "Any picture you can imagine. Just come up with something to paint," I plead. I reach for a blank canvas and place it on the easel.

Tyler lowers himself onto the stool in front of the easel. He glances at me before he turns and stares at the blank canvas, appearing completely lost.

"Okay, stop," Daphne insists, as she steps in front of me appearing determined. "I need to talk to you right now," she emphasizes, leaving no room for argument.

My eyes avert to Tyler and I apprise him, "I'll be right back."

He nods in acknowledgement and readjusts, trying to get more comfortable on the stool. He starts playing with the paintbrush in his hand as he stares blankly at the canvas.

Daphne stalks out into the front of the shop, and I reluctantly follow behind with a sigh. She takes a few steps into the middle of the room, before she spins on her heel, facing me and stopping me short. She narrows her eyes, glaring at me and my eyebrows draw down in confusion. "Daphne, what is wrong?" I prompt.

She heaves a sigh and shakes her head in disapproval. "What are you doing?" she demands.

"Huh?" I prod, not sure what she's talking about.

"What are you doing?" she repeats, dragging out each word for emphasis.

"I don't know what you mean," I proclaim, innocently.

"Noelle Palmer, you are acting like a crazy person," she boldly declares. "You are self-sabotaging," she adds in exasperation.

I shake my head in denial. She just doesn't understand. "I am painting the future, Daph," I restate. That's what's crazy, not me.

"Do you hear yourself?" she challenges, with clear disbelief. She shakes her head and continues, not waiting for my response. "You can't literally paint the future. Two weeks ago, you were terrified no one was going to come into your store," she reminds me. "Then you literally sold over ten thousand dollars on opening night," she reminds me, the pride in her voice obvious.

"What does that have to do with anything?" I challenge. I don't understand where she's trying to go with this conversation or why we have to talk about whatever it is right now. I should be helping Tyler, not standing out here wasting time.

"I'm not finished," she scolds me, causing my eyes to widen in surprise. "Five months ago, you had your heart broken. You told me then, no one would ever love you again. Now, you've got an amazing guy following you all over town and you're pushing him away," she emphasizes.

My stomach churns anxiously, but I refuse to believe she's right. "But," I attempt to interrupt.

She puts her hand up to stop me again. "I'm not done, yet," she reiterates, firmly. "It hasn't snowed the entire winter season and a lot of businesses here are really struggling. You may not understand because you're a new business owner. But without ski tourism, these places can barely keep their doors open. I'm sure Cuppa' Joe was probably doing a lot better last year at this time, but Tyler wouldn't know that because he's new too. I was talking to Sadie at the restaurant, and they might have to close next month because they can't pay their overhead. It's the same for Flannery's Pub and the bed and breakfast. I mean, even Wintergreen Inn is having trouble," she elaborates. "Do you understand what I'm saying?" she questions.

I open my mouth to respond, but I'm not sure how to answer. I feel terrible all the businesses in town seem to be struggling, but I'm still not exactly sure what she's trying to tell me by overloading me with all this discouraging and heartbreaking information. I finally shake my head, needing her to spell it out for me. "What?" I prod.

"Noelle, you are stubborn," she affirms. The corners of my mouth twitch up in amusement, knowing she's one of the few people who can say that to me, without offending me. I still feel a little apprehensive, though. My anxiety causes me to grimace, as I wait for her to continue. "You have everything right in front of you, but you keep focusing on things that don't matter, instead of seeing your own," she pauses trying to think of how she wants to phrase it, "your own gift," she finally stresses. "You have true artistic ability. You're just obsessed with an object given to you by a stranger. I just wish you could see yourself the way that we all see you," she pleads. "Accept the gifts that you're given and embrace the ones that you already have," she states, emphatically.

She's right. That's exactly what I'm doing. I'm focusing on what's causing the magic and why me, instead of creating my own magic in my artwork, in myself and in my life. Things like a special paintbrush don't matter, but the people that are important to me are what makes all the difference, people like Daphne and my family. And maybe even Tyler, if I haven't already scared him away with my theatrics. I grimace and shake my head at myself in disappointment as I reflect on my erratic behavior the past twenty-four hours. I'm such a fool. I take a step towards Daphne, with a small, appreciative smile on my face and wrap my arms around her. She immediately hugs me back and my heart clenches with love for my best friend making my chest feel tight. "I love you, Daph," I murmur, as tears well in my eyes.

She steps back and looks at me with a satisfied grin. "Right back at ya'," she mumbles, her own eyes filling with tears. I blink, a couple tears slipping out of the corners of my eyes, as I look at her feeling both grateful and apologetic. I'm so happy to have her in my life. I don't know what I'd do without a best friend like her. We both wipe the tears out of the corners of our eyes with a genuine smile towards one another. "I'll see you later," she states. Then, she turns towards the front door, calling out over her shoulder, "Goodbye."

"Bye," I reply, giving her a small wave as I watch her walk out of the shop. Then, I turn around and saunter back towards the art studio, biting my lower lip anxiously.

Daphne's right. I think I lost confidence in myself, but with the support of everyone around me and opening night going so well, I'm starting to believe in myself again. Plus, recently, I've been so focused on forgetting about my ex-boyfriend and trying to build a future for myself with the opening of the store, that I'm pushing a possible future away. I know it's not a guarantee, but isn't it worth the risk? "He's worth the risk," I mumble to myself answering my own question.

I take a deep breath and square my shoulders feigning confidence. I need to talk to Tyler. The way I've been acting, I wonder if he will even want to go on a date with me anymore. If Tyler's the kind of man he seems to be, I'm sure he'll give me a second chance; at least I hope so. I bite my lower lip and slowly release it, a small smile beginning to light up my face. A feeling of hope washes over me, as I stride back into my art studio with a new sense of determination and self-assurance. I've got this.

Chapter 18

Tyler

I tap the hard end of the paintbrush against my leg over and over again, like the beat of a drum, as I stare at the blank canvas. I wish I could do something to help Noelle, but I don't think this is it. I don't have any idea what to paint and whatever I would try to paint wouldn't appear anything like the real thing. I'm not a painter. I'm not even an artist. If anything, I might be more of a stick figure kind of guy. I sigh heavily as my shoulders sag in defeat. I like this girl and I definitely feel a strong connection with her, but I feel like I'm already letting her down or maybe she's just pushing me away.

Noelle has so much going for her. She's incredibly beautiful and so smart. She's obviously talented, and very sweet. Plus, she has the strength, dedication, courage and determination to open her own shop with things she created with her hands, mind, heart and soul. That alone is astounding. She has a lot of spunk, too. I like that about her. I grin, thinking about Noelle.

My eyes drift back to the paintbrush in my hand making me grimace. Her energy seems a bit displaced and I'm not sure how to help her quell it. No, that's not what I would want. Like I said, I like that about her. I just want to help her get her energy to change direction. It feels as if she's already looking for a reason to push me away and I'm afraid not being able to do this for her will do exactly that. How can I get to know her better, if she doesn't even give me a chance? I know I have so much left to learn about her, but I want my opportunity. Hopefully, she'll give it to me, even without me trying to paint something for her.

Noelle slowly walks back into the room, appearing as if she's deep in thought. Gathering my courage, I immediately shake my head, hoping she'll understand, but I can't do this. This isn't me and I can't pretend it is, not even for her. And besides, I really don't think it's the right thing, even if I'm not exactly sure what is. "Noelle," I begin, my tone pleading, "I really don't know anything about painting."

She flinches slightly at the sound of her name. My stomach twists, already on edge as I await her response. She closes her eyes slowly and takes a deep breath, while I hold mine. I watch as her eyes flutter open, appearing clearer than before. She meets my gaze, her blue eyes turning soft, just before she does something completely unexpected. "I'm sorry," she apologizes, sincerely.

I suck in a quick breath and tilt my head to the side as my eyebrows draw down in confusion. "For what?" I prompt, needing clarification. This feels like a complete one-eighty.

She winces and scrunches up her nose adorably, causing my heart to skip a beat. "For being a little crazy there," she grumbles. She purses her lips in thought, as she pauses. Then she exhales slowly and quietly admits, "I'm overwhelmed."

I exhale slowly, feeling my whole body relax with relief, as understanding washes over me. She has a lot going on with opening her new store, designing and creating the majority of her products and then also being responsible for all the marketing, including a big grand opening party for The First Noelle. Plus, the whole town is worried about not having any snow because it decreases the winter business this town depends on. That's not something you want to hear as a new business owner. I know she also has her family and friends to think about. Then you add this magical situation she's in and that makes everything even more complicated. I should be the last thing she's thinking about. I can't let this be about me. It's not about me, unless I spin it that way and I won't do that to her.

I stand up and set the paintbrush down next to the easel, feeling slightly relieved I don't have to paint anything to help her feel better. I nod my head as I turn back towards her with a reassuring smile. "Yeah, I can understand that," I easily concede. Any new business is a lot to take on. It's a lot of hard work, not just physically, but emotionally as well. I imagine that's especially true where creativity is essential just to remain in business. I'm sure everything she sells feels exceedingly personal to her, making it hard to let it go. I don't know if I could do it. Honestly, now that I think about it, the thought just makes me admire her even more. It seems the more I learn, the more I like about her. I can't help but think that everything about this shop, about Noelle, is immensely extraordinary. I feel a tingling sensation starting inside my chest and rapidly spreading, completely overwhelming me as I look down at her with a feeling of utter respect and awe.

"And," she continues, "I'm really glad I met you," she admits. My heart stutters in response. A small, optimistic smile plays upon her lips, as she glances up at me from underneath her long eyelashes.

I offer her a crooked grin in return; happy with where this conversation seems to be going. "Yeah?" I prompt. I arch my eyebrows in question, encouraging her to elaborate.

She nods her head in confirmation, as her cheeks turn a beautiful shade of pink at her confession. "Yeah," she confirms, giving me a somewhat timid, but hopeful look. "Life has been a lot lately and this whole paintbrush thing is freaking me out," she concedes, with a shutter.

I nod in understanding. It's a lot for me to take in too. It would be for anyone, but maybe I can still help support her if she'll let me. I believe she's worth it all. I attempt to encourage her and suggest, "Maybe you just need to relax." I take a small step towards her and look down into her pale blue eyes. "What if I take you to dinner tonight?" I propose, the corners of my mouth tugging upwards.

"Yes," she promptly replies, nodding her head in agreement. My smile instantly broadens, and tingles of excitement shoot down my spine. She finally said yes, without any hesitation. She abruptly groans in annoyance and changes her mind. "No," she corrects, with a grimace. The smile falls from my lips and my heart drops like lead to the pit of my stomach, as she shakes her head. Confused, I hold my breath and wait for her to explain why she had such a quick change of heart. I don't want to jump to conclusions before I hear what she has to say. "I have the celebration dinner tonight for my brother with my family," she explains.

My body instantly relaxes, as I nod in acknowledgement. "That's right," I mumble under my breath. She did tell me they were having dinner to celebrate her brother's win, but I seem to keep forgetting about that as well. It almost feels as if today isn't even the same day as her brother's hockey game. So much has happened since we left the rink. Then again, I also feel as if I've known Noelle a lot longer than just a couple days.

"What time is it?" she inquires, interrupting my thoughts.

I bend my arm as I flip my wrist towards my face and glance at my watch. "Four-thirty," I announce.

She nods in acknowledgement and mumbles, "Okay." She purses her lips in thought. After a moment she nods again and murmurs, "We have enough time."

My eyebrows draw down in confusion. "For what?" I prod, perplexed.

She smiles up at me, her eyes sparkling like diamonds. My heart jumps up into my throat and I immediately gulp it down. My reaction to this woman is unbelievably vast. How does she do that with just a simple smile? "I have an idea," she happily announces. "Meet me here at seven-thirty, okay?" she requests.

"For what?" I prompt, hoping she'll tell me what she's thinking. I know I'll be here either way, but it doesn't hurt to ask.

She smiles mischievously up at me, and I can't help but grin back at her expression. "For our date, of course," she declares.

My head falls back as I laugh in response, while tingles of excitement spread throughout my entire body. I'm definitely not saying no to a date with her, no matter what she wants to do. Isn't that what I've been trying to make happen since the moment I met her? Maybe this time we can make this date happen the way we'd both like it to. I chuckle softly and shake my head, still confused, but thrilled with her declaration. "I don't think I'm ever going to understand you," I blurt out, honestly.

She grins, broadly, practically bouncing with contained excitement. "Don't worry. You don't have to," she claims, feistily.

I chuckle in response. I may not have to, but I absolutely want to know her and understand her better, but isn't that what dates are for? To say Noelle intrigues me is an understatement. I have to do something to get my mind off our date later or my curiosity may get the best of me. "Can I still have these paintings?" I question, gesturing to the stack of paintings on the small table she handed me earlier.

"Not the hockey one," she informs me. "That's for my brother," she adds.

"Good," I mumble. I'm glad she's going to give the hockey painting to her brother. She did make it for him, not me and it seems like the perfect gift for him. I know she was just panicking, but I didn't feel comfortable with accepting it. I smile down at her, grateful she sounds like she feeling so much better, than she did earlier.

"Here," she offers, handing me the other two paintings.

I gently grab the canvases from her hand, being careful not to touch any of the wet paint. My fingers lightly brush hers in the exchange. I bite the inside of my cheek, as heat shoots through me like a bolt of lightning. Her soft gasp tells me, I'm not the only one feeling such a strong reaction from the subtle contact. I smile appreciatively down at her, holding her gaze as long as she'll allow it. "Thanks," I murmur, truly grateful.

"Just be careful," she warns me. "It's still wet," she emphasizes, gesturing towards both paintings in my hands.

I glance down at the paintings. I didn't realize paintings took so long to dry. I thought the cookie painting would be completely dry by now. I carefully readjust the canvases, so I'm holding both of them by the edges and away from my clothes. Then, I lift my gaze and nod my head in affirmation. "Will do," I concur.

I turn around and walk out of her studio clasping the paintings, careful not to bump into anything on the way out. I think I want to hang both of them at Cuppa Joe. Noelle really is an amazing artist. I enjoyed looking around her shop to see the various projects she worked on, including jewelry, clay vases, decorations, purses and so much more, but her paintings, in particular, have a special place in my heart. These paintings specifically have a special meaning, at least to me they do. They not only remind me of her, but also how we first met, with a little bit of magic bringing us closer together.

I smile to myself as I make my way back to the coffee shop. I'm anxious to find a good spot for these paintings. I wonder what Noelle will think when she sees her artwork displayed on the walls next time she comes into the café. I smile to myself as I maneuver the paintings and carefully pull the back door of Cuppa' Joe open, the scent of coffee, immediately filling my senses. I step inside and the door instantly bangs shut behind me. I find Mandy putting a stack of travel coffee cups and lids next to the machine. "Hi, Mandy," I greet her, again.

"Everything okay?" she asks. "You ran out of here pretty quickly and Noelle looked like she had seen a ghost," she adds.

I smile and nod my head in response. "Yeah," I answer. "Everything is great!" I declare. "There was just something important Noelle forgot to take care of," I tell her as explanation for both of us.

Her eyes narrow with curiosity. "That's good," she murmurs. "Mrs. Halsen wanted me to thank you again," she informs me. I smile in acceptance. "Nice paintings," she comments, arching her eyebrows in question.

I look down at the paintings in my hands and grin. "Thanks," I murmur. I know she's curious about the one of me holding the ring, but she knows more than most. The rest of the story is just for Noelle and me. I walk around to the tables and set both paintings down, next to one another, so I don't ruin the paint. Then I make my way to the back closet and pull it open, easily finding the red toolbox. I flip the lid open and reach inside, grabbing a hammer and a few nails, before I snap the lid closed and shut the door. I turn back to Mandy and request, "Would you help me decide where I should hang them?"

"Sure, I'd love to," she claims, nodding in agreement. She throws away the plastic that was holding the coffee lids and follows me.

"Thank you," I acknowledge, as we make our way over to the customer table where I left the paintings. "After this, I have to run to my aunt and uncle's house to help them with dinner," I inform her, "So I'll be out of your hair for the night."

She smirks and nods in acknowledgement, "Okay. Thanks for coming in to help out," she adds, gratefully. "It was a pleasant and unexpected surprise."

I smile in response as I set down the hammer and nails. "You're welcome," I murmur. Then I pick up the painting of the chocolate chip cookies first, the painting that started it all. I can't stop smiling to myself as I walk around, holding the small canvas up in a few different locations, trying to decide on the best spot for everyone to enjoy it. "I think that's perfect," Mandy advises.

"I think you're right," I concur. I grab the hammer and a nail as I allow my mind to wander to my date with Noelle, planned for later tonight. I'm incredibly eager to finally go out with her on something that feels more like a date. I wonder what she's thinking we'll do. The look on her face when she mentioned a date, gave me the impression she has something particular in mind, and I can't wait to find out what it will be! Then again, I don't think it matters what we do, as long as I get to spend more time with her.

Chapter 19

Noelle

I'm sitting at our large, round, light oak kitchen table, with Jackie on my right and Dylan on left, eating our celebration dinner with my family. Dylan changed out of his uniform into more comfortable clothes, now wearing blue jeans, a black t-shirt and a black and green checkered flannel, and my mom changed into a black turtleneck sweater after preparing dinner.

While Dylan and Dad continue to go over the details of the game, play by play, my eyes roam around the room, taking in all the Christmas decorations. Mom always makes sure to decorate every room for the holidays, making it feel like Christmas everywhere around our house. Right behind me, she has the large picture window looking out into our backyard draped with thick, green garland, wrapped with white twinkle lights. Although, right now, we can't see anything outside except the darkness of night, in the daytime we have a deep backyard with gardens along the borders and trees scattered throughout. The doorways on each end of our country-style kitchen are adorned with the same thick, green garland. On the opposite side of the kitchen, the black appliances stand amongst the cream kitchen cabinets. The under the cabinet lighting is turned on low, to help accent more of the holiday accessories. Then, she dressed the gold, tan and black countertops with a small porcelain snowman, a wooden nutcracker, a mini Christmas tree, a ceramic angel, beautifully lit and a stuffed Santa. The large, square kitchen island remains clear, except for a large, white and red platter with a snowman painted in the middle of it resting in the center, waiting for use. Seeing it sitting out makes me wonder what mom and dad have planned for dessert. They always like to celebrate special occasions with a special dessert, and I know this absolutely qualifies as one of those times.

I glance across the table at mom, sitting between Dylan and dad. "The house looks really nice, Mom. You did a great job on the Christmas decorations," I compliment her. I feel bad I wasn't any help this year, but I have been so busy with everything for The First Noelle and the grand opening celebration, that I have barely been home.

"Thank you," she acknowledges, smiling appreciatively.

"Hey, I helped," Jackie volunteers.

I chuckle in response. Mom nods her head in agreement, appeasing Jackie. She reaffirms, "Yes, Jackie helped with most of it."

I turn to my sister and offer her the compliment she's obviously searching for, "Nice job, Jackie." She grins in satisfaction, causing me to huff another laugh, but I am also grateful mom didn't do everything by herself.

I glance down at the table, covered with a white tablecloth, evergreen placemats and our white dishes, accented with a thick dark green stripe around the edges and take one more bite of the lasagna. "Mm," I moan, and set my fork down, feeling completely full.

"Alright," dad begins, bringing our attention to him. "Now that we're all done eating, I have to slip out and run a quick errand before dessert," he notifies us. "That is, if all of you can wait a few extra minutes," he teases, his lips twitching up in amusement. I smirk in response as Dylan groans quietly under his breath and Jackie giggles.

"We'll see you in a few minutes," Mom responds, instantly. She watches him as he pushes his chair back, letting the wood scrape across the floor. He stands up and she tilts her head up to look at him.

He slides his chair back into the table, sets his napkin down next to his plate and then takes a step closer to mom. He leans down towards her and kisses her sweetly on the corner of her mouth. I admire their relationship. It's the kind of marriage that seems open, honest and truly loving. I hope I'm fortunate enough to have that kind of man in my life one day. The thought again, makes my mind drift to Tyler, wondering if he could be that man. I take a deep breath and refocus on my family as my dad grins and waves goodbye to all of us. "Be right back," he adds, cheerfully. He turns and walks towards the front of the house to leave.

"Bye, Dad," Jackie, Dylan and I all call out to him, just before we hear the front door close with a thump.

"Thanks for making lasagna, Mom," Dylan mumbles, gratefully. He wipes his mouth with his napkin and sets it down on the table next to his plate.

"It was so good," Jackie raves.

Mom smiles proudly as she looks over at Dylan. "Only the best for my little champion," she praises, knowing it's one of his favorite meals. Then, she runs her fingers adoringly over the back of Dylan's hair. He leans away from her, grinning, showing me he appreciates her praise more than he wants to let on. I look down at my lap to hide my laugh at the gesture.

After a moment, I lift my gaze and turn my head, looking at my brother. "That really was one heck of a shot, Dyl," I compliment him.

He beams, full of satisfaction. "Thanks," he murmurs, appreciatively. "It felt really good," he confesses. "I'll never forget it," he admits reverently, as if on cue.

With his comment, I can't help but think this might be the perfect time to give him his gift. I realize it's not

Christmas, but it's almost like he set it up perfectly for me and I have to take advantage of the opportunity. I stand up, pushing my chair back and listening to it scrape across the floor. I place my hands on the back of my chair and smile mischievously, as I focus on my brother. "Actually," I begin, as I lean on my hands towards him, "I made sure you'll never forget it," I proclaim.

I feel everyone's curious eyes turn to me, as his eyebrows draw down in confusion. "What do you mean?" he questions.

I grin and let my hands slide off the chair as I turn around and walk away without answering him. I stride into the mudroom, just off the kitchen and open the cabinet where I hid the painting I made for him. "Noelle?" Jackie calls, sounding puzzled.

"Hang on," I reply. "I have a surprise for Dylan," I inform them, calling to them from the other room. I pull the painting out and double check to make sure I didn't leave any paint behind. Then, I hold it up in front of me, making sure everything still looks just how I want it.

"Other than the surprise from Blarney's that Dad is picking up?" Dylan prompts. I even hear the smirk in his voice from in here, making me laugh. I guess that's what we're having for dessert.

"Dylan," mom scolds. "How did you know?" she prompts, sounding curious and only slightly disappointed.

I hear the smile in his voice as he answers her. "Mrs. Blarney called and asked for my jersey number for the cake," he apprises her, chuckling softly.

"Typical," Jackie grumbles in annoyance.

I close the cabinet and step back into the room, holding the hockey painting of Dylan in celebration on the ice, right after he scored the final goal. I take a deep breath in nervous anticipation just before I turn it around and hold it up in front of me for all of them to see, my nerves instantly causing my stomach to begin churning like a hurricane. "Congratulations, Dylan!" I announce, with a small smile on my face. I bite my bottom lip and hold my breath as I anxiously wait for his reaction.

Dylan's eyes widen and he jumps to his feet in excitement. He pushes his chair back so fast, it screeches loudly across the floor and rocks back and forth, landing with a bang. "Holy crap!" he exclaims.

"Dylan!" mom instantly scolds him.

He grimaces and corrects himself a slight smirk on his face. "I mean, wow, Noelle. That's awesome," he declares. His grin widens, spreading from ear to ear.

I exhale slowly feeling relief flood my veins. My smile grows, while I enjoy his reaction. He reaches out for the painting and I quickly warn him, "Be careful. It's still wet."

He nods in acknowledgement as he stares at the painting in awe. "Okay," he mumbles, inaudibly under his breath. He cautiously takes the painting from me, gripping it gently around the edges. Watching him treat it like a prized possession causes my chest to tighten and a lump to form in my throat. He holds it out in front of him, looking at it with utter appreciation and awe.

I glance at my mom and realize her mouth is slightly open in shock. Shaking her head, she prods, "How did you paint that so fast?"

I again attempt to gulp down the lump in my throat and open my mouth to respond, but I immediately snap it closed, taking another deep breath to quell my emotions trying to overtake me. "You must have a magic paintbrush or something," Jackie comments, sarcastically, shaking her head in wonder.

Her comment elicits a giggle from my lips, as chills spread over my whole body, but the remark also makes me feel lighter. Afterall, I was the one who created it. I just did it this morning, not this afternoon like they think. If the paintbrush really is magic, it didn't do the actual work to create the painting. That part was all me. "Something like that," I mumble my agreement, as an overwhelming feeling of pride washes over me.

"Thank you," Dylan proclaims, happily. "This is awesome," he reiterates.

I smile, gratefully. "I'm glad you like it," I admit, knowing that's putting it mildly. I've never seen Dylan this excited about any of my work before. It really means a lot to me. "I was going to give it to you for Christmas, but this seemed more appropriate," I enlighten him.

He sets the painting down on the seat of his chair and unexpectedly throws his arms around me, hugging me tightly. I gasp in surprise and lift my arms, wrapping them around my brother and hug him back, a rush of warmth spreading through me. I can't help but smile to myself, feeling grateful and enjoying the moment. "Thank you, Noelle," he rasps. "You don't know what this means to me," he contends, sounding a little choked up, while still shaking his head in disbelief.

I pat my brother gently on the back as I take my own deep, calming breath. He's rarely this emotional about something. I'm thrilled I was able to do this for him. I can't believe I almost gave this one away. I quickly shove the thought away, trying to remain in the moment with my brother. "Don't go getting soft on me, Kid," I tease him, attempting to bring the focus away from me and fully on him. We both slowly drop our arms from around each other and take a step back. "You've got a real gift for hockey, Dylan," I claim, offering him another compliment.

"You can say that, again," Mom asserts, smiling at the two of us with pure pleasure lighting up her face.

Dylan laughs and discreetly wipes the corners of his eyes, while we all pretend not to notice. "This is the best gift I've ever gotten," he reiterates, emphatically.

"Really?" I question, my own heart clenching with his words. "You like it that much?" I prompt, needing clarification. I bite my lower lip in anticipation of his response. I'm not really looking for him to say anymore, but this much of a compliment isn't normally something I would hear from my brother, and it means more to me than I can even express. I feel an overwhelming sense of confidence and satisfaction wash over me with Dylan's praise.

He smirks, with a mischievous glint in his eyes. He tilts his head to the side and glances at me, his eyes sparkling with amusement at my question. He finally shrugs his shoulders and carelessly mumbles, "Eh, don't let it go to your head." We all burst out laughing in response. At the same time, his comment helps bring us all back to our normal.

As we quiet down, my shoulders begin to relax. I feel so much better about my gift for him, even if some of it is magic in a way. Is that really so bad? I could do a lot of good with just a little bit of magic.

I shake my head in realization as the thought reminds me of Tyler. It seems I should've been listening to him all along. I glance up at the round, black and white clock, mounted on the wall above the back door, to check the time. Then, I look across the table at my mom, changing the subject. "Mom, do you mind if I don't clean up after dinner?" I request, pleading with her with my eyes. When she doesn't answer right away I announce, "I have a date."

"Ooh," Jackie grins, playfully. She's barely able to sit still at my news. "With that scorekeeper guy?" she prods, arching her eyebrows in question.

I feel the heat rush to my cheeks, immediately turning them pink, as I nod in confirmation. "Tyler. Yes," I murmur.

A wide grin covers my mom's face, as she encourages, "Go ahead, Noelle."

"I'll clean up for you," Jackie offers.

"Thank you," I mumble in appreciation. I don't want to mess up anything with Tyler again after everything I've put him through in the last two days. Plus, I have something I want to take care of before he comes to meet me.

"And I'll eat your dessert for you," Dylan adds, grinning at his offer.

I roll my eyes, barely fighting a smile. "That's so kind of you, Dylan," I joke, thick on my sarcasm.

"That's me," he replies, smugly.

I chuckle softly at his antics. Mom gives Dylan a pointed look before bringing her attention back to me. "I'll save you a piece, Noelle," she proclaims.

"Thanks, Mom!" I respond. Then I push my chair into the table. "Tell Dad I promise I won't be late," I claim.

"I will," mom agrees, with a firm nod of her head.

"Bye," I convey to all three of them as I wave.

"Bye," they all reply.

Then, I immediately stride towards the front of the house, grabbing my coat off the front hook and quickly slip it on. I reach into the pockets, making sure my keys are still there, my fingertips connecting with the jagged, cold metal. I grab my phone out of my back pocket and glance at the time again, before I slip it into my empty coat pocket. I better hurry if I want to try to get this started and close to done before Tyler shows up at the shop. Plus, I definitely don't want tonight to turn into another non-date for any reason. Tyler deserves all my attention tonight. I open the front door and step outside into the cool, crisp night air. I pull the door shut behind me with a bang and make my way down my steep driveway, turning towards town, Main Street and The First Noelle. I walk as quickly as I can, not wanting to waste a minute, as I let my idea slowly formulate in my head. I may not have any expectations for how my painting will turn out, but this time, I'm so excited to see what happens when it's finished.

Chapter 20

Noelle

I find myself in a place inside my new shop that's rapidly becoming extremely familiar, standing in front of my easel holding a blank canvas in my quaint art studio. I smile to myself as I paint, feeling better about my magic paintbrush. Isn't this a good thing? I'm sure most people would love to be in a position to truly make a difference and really help people. I'm in that exact situation right now and there's no way I'm going to let my insecurities get the better of me and allow it to pass me by. It's my turn to attempt to make an impact in my community. The ironic thing to me is that I'm able to do that by simply doing what I love, painting.

I touch the brush to the blank canvas, easily filling it in with an array of color. The view I'm portraying is someone else's point of view, as if they're looking at me from behind. The painted image of myself, wearing the same clothes I'm wearing now, peers out the window of my art studio. I have no idea if this will even work, but if this paintbrush is truly magical, then without a doubt, it's worth a try. Besides, I believe it's better for me to put this brush to good use, instead of stressing about the pressure and panicking, like I did earlier. I understand now, why this paintbrush is such a special gift. I can help so many people with this painting alone, that is, if it works. Hopefully, my painting could even help make dreams come true. I've always put so much of myself into my work, but this feels as if it adds even more of my heart and soul into it with its touch of magic. I sigh happily, as I quickly become lost in my work.

It feels as if only a few minutes have passed when the chimes ring, indicating someone just entered in through the front door of my shop. I glance through the window of my art studio into the interior of the store and smile at Tyler approaching. I set down my paint palette, now prepared with white paint, along with the magic paintbrush, laying them gently on the shelf. Then I walk out to meet him as he advances towards me. He meets my gaze and grins broadly, his bright smile giving me goose bumps. "Hi," he murmurs, in greeting.

"Hi," I whisper as I exhale, the corners of my lips curving upwards. "Lock the door, would you?" I request.

"Okay," he instantly agrees. "Are you ready for our date?" he inquires, as he turns back around towards the front door. He takes two steps, flips the lock on the door until it clicks in place and then spins back to me.

I smile, anxiously and begin to fidget, clasping and twisting my hands together nervously. "I actually have something to show you that I've been working on, first," I prompt. I bite my lower lip, awaiting his reaction, as he closes the distance between us. I have no idea what he will think of this.

His eyebrows draw down in confusion, as he looks me in the eyes, assessing me, as if trying to read my mind. "Okay," he mutters, dragging out the word.

My heart pounds in anticipation and at the same time, gives me the boost I need to suddenly regain my confidence. "Come with me," I instruct. I spin on my heel and stride back into my art studio. I stop in front of the painting I've been working on and stare at it with a small smile playing on my lips.

Tyler steps up next to me and tilts his head to the side, considering my nearly finished painting. "What's this?" he prods curiously.

"What do you think it is?" I challenge him. I bite my bottom lip in eagerness, waiting for his answer.

He turns and looks out the window and then twists back to me. "It's you painting in front of your window?" he questions, gesturing towards the large picture window behind us.

I give my head a firm nod in confirmation. "Exactly," I announce, a pleased smile on my face. I pick up the paintbrush along with the palette I prepared with the white paint. Then I stand in front of the easel.

Tyler's eyebrows draw down in confusion. He looks back and forth between the easel, the window and then back to me. "I don't get it," he concedes.

I take a deep breath to calm my nerves and exhale slowly before I begin my explanation. "Well, Daphne made me realize that everything that has happened to me over the past few days is truly a gift. From this paintbrush," I hold up the paintbrush in my hand, "to meeting you," I add, quietly. I feel the heat rush to my cheeks instantly with my admission.

Tyler smiles down at me, his green eyes sparkling as he moves a little closer to me. He playfully prods, "I like where this is going."

I grin wider and feel myself blush an even deeper shade of red. Clearing my throat, I quickly continue, pushing through my anxiety and hoping I don't forget what I want to say to him. "She also made me realize that everyone in this town is struggling and I've got it really good. I've been really, really lucky," I emphasize. Tyler nods his head in acknowledgement, since it's something we've talked about before too. I turn away from him and back towards my painting. I think the easiest thing would be to show him what I'm trying to do.

I lift the paintbrush and dip it gently into the white paint on my palette. I tap it lightly to make sure just the right amount of paint sits on the tip. Then, I hold the paintbrush up to my painting, right where the glass of the window is and add snowflakes, making it appear as if it's snowing just outside my window while I paint.

"What are you doing?" Tyler prompts, curious.

I glance up at him, the corners of my mouth twitching up. "I'm adding a little bit of Christmas magic," I reveal confidently.

"Snow?" he prods, arching his eyebrows.

I give him a firm nod in confirmation. "Snow," I declare.

I finish adding snowflakes to the canvas and then I glance up at Tyler with hopeful anticipation. His gaze slides from my painting to me, a small smile tugging at his lips, before he looks out the window. His eyes narrow briefly trying to get a better look at what he's seeing. He gasps softly. "No way," he mumbles, in utter surprise.

I glance up and inhale quickly in shock, my hand reaching for my chest as snowflakes begin falling right outside my window. It's actually snowing! Warmth floods me knowing how much good this can do. This may be something that seems so small, but it will make such a huge impact on our town and everyone in our community. "It worked," I murmur, quietly, momentarily stunned.

"This can't be happening," he mumbles, in near disbelief.

I throw my arms around Tyler's neck, still holding the paintbrush, but careful not to get any paint on him. He returns my hug, his hands wrapping around my back slowly, obviously a little astounded, but relishing our embrace. I release him, letting my hands fall to my sides. Looking into his eyes, I exclaim, "It worked!" I feel the excitement growing inside of me making it nearly impossible to sit still. "Come on!" I encourage. I grab Tyler's hand and gently tug him out of the studio with me. He stumbles behind me, as I pull him through my shop and out the back door, a bounce in every move I make. The moment we step outside I drop his hand and hold my arms out as I look up at the sky, pure happiness radiating from every part of me. We both spin slowly around, looking up at the sky in awe, as snowflakes float down from the clouds falling all around us.

"It's actually snowing," Tyler reaffirms, still dumbfounded.

I giggle in response, completely elated. "It worked!" I joyfully reiterate. I stop spinning and focus my attention on Tyler, beaming gleefully at him. He grins and shakes his head in amazement as he watches me enjoying the moment. "Let's go see Daphne," I urge.

"Okay," he concurs, nodding his head in agreement.

We quietly walk towards Daphne's shop, side by side. I continue looking all around me, trying to take in the reality of the snow falling all around us. Just before we reach Daphne's Doggie Palace, we spot her running towards us, accompanied by a big golden retriever attached to a thick, red leash. "Noelle, Noelle!" she calls out to me to get our attention the moment she sees us approaching.

"Daph!" I yell. "It's snowing!" I giddily declare.

"Did you paint it?" she inquires.

I grin and nod my head in confirmation. "I did," I announce proudly.

"It worked?" she challenges, her eyes wide with surprise, even though she already knows the answer.

I nod my head as another giggle escapes my lips. "It worked," I confirm.

She throws her arms around me in a tight hug, and I happily squeeze her back. Then she releases me and takes a step back, her excitement palpable. The dog suddenly jumps up on me, as if wanting to join in on our delight. I lose my balance and feel the paintbrush being knocked out of my hand. I gasp and attempt to hold on tight, but it's no use. I didn't even realize I was still holding it. "Bailey, No!" Daphne scolds, pulling the dog back. I watch, completely helpless as the paintbrush slips out of my fingers and clatters to the ground. It bounces into the street, just as a shiny, cherry red Jeep comes around the corner driving straight for us.

"No!" I yell. I feel the panic surge up my throat and out to my limbs. I attempt to lurch towards the paintbrush to save it before the Jeep runs it over and destroys it.

"No, Noelle!" Tyler screams, but I don't even register his warning. He swiftly wraps his arm around my waist from behind and yanks me back to the safety of the sidewalk. He momentarily holds me protectively against his chest, our hearts pounding as we watch helplessly, while the car drives over the paintbrush.

I flinch at the sound of the simple crack of the wood, as my paintbrush is completely shattered under the Jeep. My heart jumps up to my throat and then drops to the pit of my stomach. I powerlessly mutter, "Oh, no! No, no, no, no, no!" I gasp for breath as I stare at the ground and the remains of my paintbrush, feeling utterly devastated.

The car comes to a complete stop in front of us. I lift my gaze, watching as the driver's side door opens and a man with a white beard, rosy cheeks and friendly blue eyes steps out from behind the wheel. I gasp, immediately recognizing him as the man who stopped in at my shop the other day. The same man I believe left the paintbrush in my shop on the day of my grand opening. He's dressed casually in dark, blue jeans and a cherry red button-down dress shirt. I'm again amazed at how much he looks like Santa Claus to me. "You," I grumble, accusingly.

He grins broadly as he greets me. "Well, hello, Noelle! It's so good to see you again," he proclaims, cheerfully.

"Why did you do that?" I prompt, still upset about my broken paintbrush. I had just been able to straighten everything out in my mind and find my confidence again. Why did the paintbrush have to break now?

"Do what?" he probes, seeming a little puzzled.

"You ran over my paintbrush!" I announce. I gesture towards the broken paintbrush lying on the ground underneath his car.

He glances down on the ground and crouches near his front tire. He picks up a piece of the broken paintbrush, sadness washing over his face. "Oh, dear," he murmurs, regretfully, as he picks up the other two pieces.

"Noelle, it was an accident," Tyler reminds me.

"This is the man that gave it to me," I enlighten them both. I know it's the truth, without even asking him.

Tyler and Daphne both turn to the man with wide eyes and mouths open in shock. "Santa?" they ask in unison.

He chuckles heartily in response. "Ho, ho, ho. I wouldn't say that too loud if I were you," he advises.

"But you are Santa, aren't you?" I question. I need verification, although I already feel in my heart that it's true. He must be Santa.

"It doesn't really matter who I am, Noelle. Does it?" he prompts, arching his eyebrow in question.

"Well, of course," I begin.

He immediately interrupts me, giving me a slight shake of his head. "No, dear, it doesn't," he gently insists. He pauses, giving me a moment to take in what he's trying to tell me. "The important thing is that you believe in magic," he insists.

"Magic?" I repeat, trying to understand.

"What kind of magic?" Tyler probes.

"Santa?" Daphne whispers again, still staring at him in shock, her eyes as wide as saucers.

"Why all kinds of magic, Tyler," he announces.

"Tyler?" he repeats. "How do you know my name?" Tyler questions. He looks down at me, his eyebrows drawn down in confusion. "Did you tell him my name?" he probes.

I shake my head in denial and Santa laughs, ignoring his question. "There's the magic of Christmas, the magic of love and of course, the most important magic of all," he proclaims. Then he pauses and gazes towards all of us, waiting to see if we have the answer.

"The magic of Santa?" Daphne questions, as she continues staring at him with wide-eyed amazement.

"No, Daphne," he smiles kindly, and gives a small shake of his head. Then he looks at each of us before his eyes land on me. He finally gives us the answer, with complete conviction. "The magic that we all hold within ourselves. It lives in all of us," he explains.

"But, the paintbrush," I begin, shaking my head in denial. The paintbrush must've been magic.

He immediately interrupts, finishing my statement for me, "is just a paintbrush." He takes a deep breath and elaborates, "You see, Noelle, the truth is you have always had the magic deep inside you to make your own dreams come true," he enlightens me.

"I have?" I question, still feeling a small sense of doubt.

"Why didn't you just tell her that in the first place?" Tyler challenges.

Santa laughs in response, "Ho, ho, ho." He grins at Tyler and claims, "Because she wouldn't have believed me! Come on, some old man that looks like Santa Claus?" he prods challenging him, with an arch of his eyebrow. "No," he mumbles shaking his head in amusement. I know he's right. He pats my arm in encouragement and looks me in the eyes. "You needed to find that confidence within yourself," he asserts.

I nod my head in agreement, as a feeling of understanding washes over me. "Which I did when I painted the snow," I murmur, thoughtfully.

"Yes," he agrees, gleeful.

"Deep down I knew that it was going to work. I knew if I painted it snowing, it would snow, and it did," I claim. "I had faith that what I created was going to be good enough to make a difference. I believed in the magic I had within myself." I look at Santa and clarify. "Is that right?"

"It certainly is," he reaffirms, giving me a proud smile.

"But she painted things that came true!" Tyler reiterates. "The cookies, the hockey game, the ring and now the snow," he elaborates.

Santa shrugs his shoulders as if it's no big deal. "Mere coincidences," he claims. "The paintbrush isn't magic," he asserts, chuckling, "ho, ho, ho." He holds out his hands, gesturing all around him. "Could you imagine if I gave out magical gifts to everyone?" he prompts, the corners of his mouth curving up in delight. "People have to find their own magic," he emphasizes. He hands the broken pieces of the paintbrush to me with an encouraging smile. "Merry Christmas, Noelle," he announces giving me a wink of his eye.

I take the paintbrush pieces from his hand and grin back at him in appreciation. "Merry Christmas," I echo his words back to him. The three of us watch as Santa climbs back into his Jeep and buckles his seat belt. He drives away with a nod of his head and a small wave to all of us.

Daphne takes a step towards his retreating car. "Bye, Santa," she softly calls after him.

Tyler puts his arm around me, and I lean into him, still a little stunned about what just occurred. We stare in the direction the Jeep drove, until any sign of red completely disappears off in the distance. I look up at Tyler and smile at him, grateful he's still here with me, giving us a chance. He grins down at me, with his green eyes sparkling, causing my heart to skip a beat and butterflies to take flight in my stomach. It feels as if everything is finally falling into place and I'm going to help make it happen.

Chapter 21

As Santa drove away, the three friends stood and stared.
They couldn't believe this new secret they shared.

The weather was wintry for the rest of the season.
And only these three, knew exactly the reason.

The ice skaters skated, the skiers, they skied.
The sledders were sledding, with the greatest of speed.

Their Christmas was white, and Santa was jolly.
For snow had returned to the hills of Mount Holly.

Tyler

I reach down and brush off my dark blue jeans, now a little damp from falling a couple times, as I awkwardly make my way off the ice and towards the benches with Noelle by my side. "So, what did you think?" she prods curiously.

I smirk and mumble, "I think I'm going to have a few new bruises tomorrow and maybe even be a little sore."

She giggles softly. "Well, I think you did really well," she praises, encouraging me.

I chuckle softly in response and shake my head in denial, glancing in her direction. She looks beautiful wearing black leggings, an oversized ivory cable knit sweater with a cowl neck underneath her familiar olive-green jacket, zipped only half-way along with ivory tight knit gloves and a matching ivory knit hat adorned with a pom-pom on top, with her long blonde hair hanging loosely out of it. "Thanks, but I know you're just being nice. Besides, I think if it's even partially true, it has a lot to do with the talented and very patient woman teaching me, or trying to, anyway," I claim.

She blushes, her already flushed skin turning a darker shade of pink. "You're sweet," she murmurs.

"Well, thank you. You make it easy," I add, honestly. "I did have a lot of fun, Noelle, even with falling a few times," I murmur, smirking as I catch her gaze. She giggles softly in response, giving me goosebumps. I take a deep breath warming my insides. I don't mind a few bumps and bruises if my reward is spending time with her. I don't ever want her to have any doubt about that.

I'm glad I dressed warm with a black long sleeved thermal, an evergreen-colored ribbed sweatshirt with a quarter-zip at my neck and my black winter coat. I wasn't quite sure what to wear, since watching a hockey game is quite different than actually skating on the ice, or at least attempting to skate, but I figured layers would be my best option.

"I had a lot of fun, too," she concurs. She smiles and breaks our gaze as she sits down and pulls her gloves off, stuffing them into her coat pockets. Then, she leans over and begins unlacing her pearly white ice skates accented with pale pink on the tongue and along the edge of the top of the boot, bleeding into the inside.

I lower myself onto the bench next to her, following suit and start unlacing the black and white ice skates on my own feet. I groan as I tug them off one by one, my feet feeling instant relief and a little sore at the same time around my ankles. I wiggle my toes and stretch my feet, trying to regain my circulation. "Does it always feel like this?" I probe.

She giggles again and glances at me as she pulls her duck boots back onto her feet. "It's just like wearing in a new pair of shoes. It takes time, but you'll get used to it."

She pauses, smirking and challenges, "That is if you're brave enough to come back."

I nod my head in confirmation and proclaim, "I'll be here for another lesson as long as you continue being my teacher."

"I can do that," she concurs. "Are you hungry?" she prompts.

I nod my head and force myself to smile. "Yeah, sure," I mumble. My stomach turns, feeling anything but ready to eat. Although, I haven't been able to stop thinking about dinner, especially knowing we're having dinner with her whole family. This is our third official date, but this is a small town and with everyone knowing everyone around here, I agreed the moment she asked, knowing it's the right thing to do and it seems I'd do about anything for her. Besides, all of them already know my family, it's my turn to get to know hers. I only met Jackie briefly after the game, but she seems nice, and I'm sure I can always talk hockey with Dylan, especially now that they won the final championship game. It's her mom and dad that I'm actually nervous about meeting.

"Don't worry," she urges. "They're going to love you," she insists, attempting to ease my anxiety about tonight.

I sit up and look over at her in wonder, just as she finishes tying her shoes and turns to me, meeting my gaze. "How do you do that?" I prompt.

"What?" she questions, a curious smile on her lips.

"Know exactly what I'm thinking and calm my nerves in the same breath. It's like you read my mind," I murmur.

She smirks and arches her eyebrows in challenge. "Maybe I did," she teases.

My head falls back as I burst into laughter, and she grins, satisfied with my response. "You're funny," I mumble, clearly amused.

"I thought so," she jokes. She stands, reaching for my skates. "I'll return these for you while you get your shoes on," she offers as she stands, with my rented skates in her hands.

"You don't have to do that. I'll just be another minute," I advise, reaching down to tug my shoes on. She keeps distracting me and slowing me down by not really doing anything but being here. I admit, I think I could stare at her all day.

"It's no problem," she reiterates, grinning. "I'll be right back." She strides towards the skate rental counter at the end of the ice, returning my skates for me, before I have a chance to argue with her any further.

I speed up my pace, quickly pulling my shoes on and tying the laces. Standing up just as she reappears in front of me. "Thank you," I proclaim appreciatively.

She loops the laces of her skates together, then slips them over her shoulder like a bag. Then she lifts her head, smiling up at me, and taking my breath away. "You're welcome," she replies. "Are you ready?" she prompts.

I gulp down the lump in my throat and nod my head in acknowledgement. "Yeah," I rasp. Clearing my throat, I prompt, "Let's go."

I reach for her hand, intertwining her warm fingers with my cold ones. The corners of her mouth twitch up as I give her hand a gentle squeeze and she returns the gesture as we walk side by side out to my car. "You should wear gloves next time," she advises.

I chuckle softly, knowing she's right, but I prod, "Are my hands too cold for you?"

She looks up at me with a smile and shakes her head in denial, "Nope, they're good. I just don't want you to be cold," she claims.

I grin at her response as we take our time strolling the rest of the way through the parking lot hand in hand, in comfortable silence. As we reach my car, I walk with her to the passenger side. I give her hand a gentle tug as I halt my footsteps, urging her to face me. I look down into her bright blue eyes, twinkling with happiness, maintaining my hold on her hand. "Do you have plans for dinner tomorrow night?"

"No," she answers. "Why?"

Ignoring her question, I ask, "Would you like to go out to dinner with me tomorrow?"

She laughs, the sound sending shivers down my spine that aren't from the cold. "Don't you think we should get through tonight first?" she prompts.

"Nope," I mumble, shaking my head. "I'd rather have a guaranteed date planned before I have dinner with your family," I declare, smirking, knowing my invite has nothing to do with her family and more to do with spending more time with her. Even when she's working, she has to make time to eat.

"You will be fine," she emphasizes.

Nodding my head, I mumble my agreement, "I know I will." She pauses, waiting for me to elaborate. "With everything I know about you, I'm sure I'll get along well with your family, but I'm nervous because I really want them to like me. I think you're beautiful, smart, talented, funny, caring, generous, brave and so much more," I compliment, enjoying the light blush of her cheeks. "I want them to know how much you already mean to me and I wonder if it might be too soon for that. The thing is, I don't need more time with you to know how special you are, Noelle. I just want it, but I'm already convinced, and we haven't even had our first kiss yet," I tease. The corners of my mouth twitch up in amusement as I watch her cheeks flood with red, giving me my desired effect.

"I know they will like you," she emphasizes, "because I know I really like you." Her words cause my chest to tighten, sending tingles throughout my body. "And Tyler, I think you're pretty incredible too," she whispers her admission, keeping it simple as she continues staring into my eyes. "As for our first kiss," she prods, trailing off. She looks up at me with a hopeful expression, causing my heart to skip a beat and my breath to catch in my throat.

I gulp hard and rasp, "Yeah?"

"I think we should remedy that right now. Don't you?" she prompts, looking at me with a mischievous glint in her eyes.

My heart begins to race as my eyes drift from her full pink lips to her inviting blue eyes, pulling me in. Her free hand reaches up and rests gently on my shoulder, curving slightly around the back of my neck, giving me goosebumps. I tilt my head down as I lift my hand, brushing a loose strand of her blonde hair out of her face. I cup her cheek as she pushes up on her tiptoes, closing the distance between us until we're barely a breath apart. I take a deep breath and exhale slowly. Then, I whisper over her lips, "I think that's a fantastic idea."

I tenderly brush my mouth over her soft lips, savoring the moment as I lose track of everything but her. She pushes forward as I tilt down further, our lips moving together in a slow, sweet rhythm, making it difficult to breathe. We slow the kiss and I pull back, looking down at her with awe, with my heart hammering against my ribcage. "Wow," she mumbles under her breath.

A small smile graces my lips as I try to catch my breath. "You can say that again," I mumble. "Kissing you was magic," I add absentmindedly.

She gasps and gently pulls back, her eyes suddenly wide with challenge. "Tyler," she warns playfully.

I laugh, realizing what I just said and shrug my shoulders like it's no big deal. How could it be when it's true? I reluctantly let my hand slip off her face and proclaim, "We should go. I don't want to be late for dinner with your family," I emphasize. "I want to make a magical impression and being late won't help me," I add playfully.

She giggles and shakes her head in amusement. Then, she heaves a sigh and nods her head, reluctantly agreeing. "You're right," she reiterates. I step back and pull the car door open, waiting as she slips her skates off her shoulder first and sets them behind the front seat. Then she lowers herself into the passenger seat. "And my answer is yes, Tyler." My eyebrows draw down in confusion, trying to remember what I asked her earlier. She smirks and reiterates, "I will go out to dinner with you tomorrow night."

I grin, my stomach twisting as warmth floods my body from the inside out feeling like things are starting to look up again. "Good," I happily proclaim. "I'm looking forward to it." I make sure she's safely tucked inside before I slam the door shut and jog around the hood of the car. I slip in behind the wheel, and pull my door closed. I glance over at her, wondering how I got so lucky. I may not have come to Mount Holly under the best of circumstances, but I'm thankful I'm here now, and not just for my family. I may joke about it, but everything really does feel magical when I'm with Noelle. She's like a bright light bringing warmth, happiness, love and laughter. My heart stutters with hope that she truly is my future. I look out the windshield and start my car, backing out of my parking space and driving towards her house with a small smile on my face, ready to meet the rest of her family.

Epilogue

Noelle

Two weeks later…

I swipe the credit card, setting it in the card holder as I finish wrapping the necklace and earrings, placing them in a gift bag and tying the handles with a thin, gold ribbon. Then, I set the bag on the counter and run my hands down the front of my outfit, while I continue waiting for the customer's credit card to process. I'm wearing black leggings, a loose-fitting, white t-shirt, a pale blue, thin, cardigan sweater that hangs open and nearly falls to my knees, gradually turning a darker shade of blue towards the bottom as well as on the ends of my sleeves. The charge finally goes through, automatically printing out the receipt. I reach up, tearing off the paper and hand him his credit card along with a receipt for him to sign and a red pen with The First Noelle written on the side of the pen in white. He quickly scrawls his name on the slip of paper, before sliding it back towards me. I reach over the counter and hand him the white gift bag, along with his receipt, offering him a grateful smile. "Happy New Year," I state.

The man grins back at me and murmurs his appreciation, "Thank you." Then he turns and strides back through the store and out the front door.

I turn my attention to the couple approaching the register. I smile broadly, instantly recognizing Mr. Carlyle, with his long, black winter coat draped over his arm. He's dressed casually in tan slacks and a brown crew-neck sweater with a navy-blue and red finely checkered patterned button-down shirt underneath with the collar folded down over the top of the sweater. Next to him, stands a tall, thin, beautiful woman with warm, toffee brown eyes, high cheekbones, a button nose and black hair, styled in a short pixie cut. She's wearing a loose-fitting burgundy silk top, draped with a matching ribbon-like tie in the middle at her neck and black dress pants with her black and white striped winter coat hanging over her arm. She must be his wife. I can't help but wonder what she thought of my painting he bought from me to give her for Christmas causing my heart to pick up its pace in anticipation.

"Noelle!" he exclaims stepping towards me. "It's so wonderful to see you!" he happily states in greeting.

I quickly make my way around the counter to welcome him and the woman standing by his side. "Happy New Year, Mr. Carlyle," I declare.

"I was hoping you would be here," he claims. "I want you to meet my wife, Janice," he adds. He glances towards his wife, grinning proudly.

I smile and hold my hand out for her to shake. She ignores my hand and leans in towards me, wrapping me up in a welcoming hug, completely taking me by surprise. "It's so lovely to meet you, Noelle," she croons.

I pat her gently on the back. Then, I take a small step backwards, as she releases me. "It's very nice to meet you, Mrs. Carlyle," I assert.

"Oh, please, call me Janice," she insists. "You are so talented," she states emphatically, complimenting me as her eyes quickly sweep the room full of amazement. Mr. Carlyle grins, nodding his head in agreement.

My heartbeat speeds up and I feel my cheeks heat in both embarrassment and appreciation. I spot Tyler approaching behind Mr. and Mrs. Carlyle from out of the corner of my eye. I smile shyly and gratefully covey, "Thank you so much."

"I absolutely adore the painting," she praises, her hand covering her heart. I feel myself relax, knowing she's referring to the painting I sold her husband of the tree on the hill. The painting of the spot they were engaged. I'm thrilled to hear how much it she loves it. I don't know if I could have let it go if it wasn't for their special story. I'm grateful to know they will both treasure it like I would, albeit for their own unique reasons, but I love that. "John tells me that he will be commissioning some of your paintings for our hotels," she prompts.

He nods in confirmation, "I certainly am."

I feel the excitement of this opportunity begin to take hold of me, feeling like I have a fire burning inside of me. I've been talking with Mr. Carlyle about the paintings he wants for the last two weeks trying to get an idea what he's looking for and what I could do for him, but every time we do, it feels a little more real to me. I nod my head in confirmation and inform her, "Yes, I will be in New York next weekend to take a look at the hotels." I've seen pictures of the hotels, but I need a better feel for the atmosphere of the hotels to decide what kind of artwork will work best with the ambiance and the best way to do that is to go there to see and experience the space in person. I can't wait.

She lays her hand gently on my forearm and leans towards me. She offers, "Then, you simply must let me take you out to dinner."

"Oh, dinner sounds absolutely lovely," I murmur, honestly. "Thank you," I add, offering her a gracious smile.

I wave to Tyler standing just off to the side, encouraging him to come closer. He steps up next to me, holding a travel cup in each hand, with steam coming out of the small opening in the top. He's wearing dark blue jeans and an olive-green pullover with two light brown buttons at his neck. He has his black, quilted winter coat pulled on over the top, but leaves it hanging open. He grins politely at all of us, his green eyes sparkling brightly making my chest tighten. "Hi," he states, greeting the three of us at once.

"Hi," I reply, a small smile curving my lips. Butterflies instantly take flight in my stomach and goosebumps cover my arms at just the sight of him. Then, I twist towards Mr. and Mrs. Carlyle to introduce them. "Mr. and Mrs. Carlyle, this is my boyfriend, Tyler," I happily announce. My stomach does a flip, enjoying the sound of saying those words aloud.

"Nice to meet you, Tyler," Mrs. Carlyle murmurs.

"Nice to meet you," John proclaims.

Tyler grins in recognition at the sound of their names. "It's nice to meet both of you as well," he declares.

"Oh," Mrs. Carlyle mumbles, an idea popping into her head as she smiles at the two of us. "You should come with Noelle to the city next weekend," she suggests to Tyler, with a quick glance in my direction.

He grins down at me. The look he gives me makes it difficult to breathe. "Maybe I will," he agrees almost instantly, without even knowing the details about the trip.

I blush and force myself to tear my eyes away from Tyler, before I get lost in his emerald gaze. I take a deep breath, bringing my attention back to Mr. and Mrs. Carlyle. He grins, looking at me and explains, "We just wanted to stop by and say hello."

Mrs. Carlyle nods her head in agreement. She happily adds, "The skiing this weekend has been absolutely incredible."

"I'm so glad you are both enjoying yourselves," I declare. "Are you going to the Town Square for the fireworks?" I inquire.

"We wouldn't miss it," Mrs. Carlyle proclaims, her excitement obvious. Mr. Carlyle nods his head in agreement, glancing fondly at his wife. My heart warms, seeing how much love the two of them have for each other. They remind me of my mom and dad. It's the kind of love I hope to have one day with my husband when I'm married. I glance at Tyler wondering again if he will be the one by my side. The thought instantly heats my whole body, my heart picking up its pace and making it difficult to catch my breath. I tear my gaze away from Tyler and take a deep breath, exhaling slowly as I quickly push the thought out of my head for now and focus on enjoying the moment.

"Thanks for coming by," I state.

"I'm really glad we did. We'll see you soon," Mr. Carlyle replies.

They both start turning towards the door, when Mrs. Carlyle stops abruptly in front of a small shadowbox with a black wooden frame about half an inch thick. Inside, the box holds the three broken pieces of the magic paintbrush. It's a simple piece that means so much to me, as well as Tyler. I wanted it to be displayed at the front of my shop to remind me daily of the magic I have inside of me and the two people that shared in the experience along with me. I'm thankful it was Daphne and Tyler by my side. It's an inspiration to me every time I catch even a glimpse of it. It also reminds me of my priorities. I don't ever want to lose sight of what's important to me again. Life is too precious. "Oh," she murmurs, admiring the piece. She takes a step towards it and reaches for it. "This is an interesting piece," she murmurs, admiring it. "How much?" she inquires, glancing over at me.

"It's not for sale," Tyler and I blurt out in unison. I feel myself blush a deep shade of red, as Tyler bites his lower lip to hold back a laugh.

Her eyes instantly widen in surprise at our quick retort. She glances at the two of us and a slow grin spreads across her face as if understanding how special the piece is to both of us. "Well, okay then," she responds with a nod of her head.

Mr. Carlyle smiles and proclaims, "Happy New Year, kids."

"You too," I reply. We watch as Mr. Carlyle puts his arm protectively around his wife and escorts her out of the shop.

Tyler turns back to me as the door closes behind them, leaving the two of us alone in my store. He holds out his right hand, offering me one of the cups. "Here," he verbalizes. "Some of Aunt Viv's special hot cocoa," he enlightens me, with a satisfied grin.

I smile gratefully up at him. Then, I reach out and take the cup from his hands, my fingers lightly brushing his in the exchange, causing tingles to shoot up my arm and my heart to skip a beat. I take a deep breath, inhaling the sweet chocolatey scent as I bring it to my mouth. I blow on it gently through the small opening and then I cautiously take a sip, not wanting to burn my tongue. The rich, chocolate taste instantly brings my taste buds to life. "Mm," I murmur, in satisfaction. "This is so good. Thank you," I mumble, appreciatively.

"You're welcome," he mumbles. He smiles down at me and nods his head in acknowledgement. Then, he takes a deep breath and changes the subject. "So, are you ready for the fireworks?" he prompts, looking hopeful.

"Do you really want to go?" I question.

"Well, Aunt Vivienne said that they are magical," he advises, the corners of his lips twitching up in amusement. Then, he gives me a slight shrug of his shoulders in response, letting me know he's leaving the choice up to me.

I smile playfully up at him and take a small step closer to him, closing the distance between us. Then, I tilt my head up towards him and look into his eyes as I proclaim, "Tyler, I've got all of the magic I need right here."

He grins down at me, his eyes sparkling with happiness. He tips his head down and gently presses his lips to mine, my lips tingling the moment we touch. He slowly moves his mouth against mine, his kiss soft and loving, completely taking my breath away. I fall back on my heels, breaking the kiss and look into his eyes. My heart skips a beat, before it starts up again, pounding hard and fast against my chest. We hear a loud bang, the sound of the fireworks starting up over Mount Holly. I smile at Tyler, and he grins adoringly back at me. I push up on my tiptoes and close the distance between us once again, pressing my lips to his, and kissing him again with my heart full. I know I'm exactly where I'm meant to be.

The fireworks display lit the sky on New Year's Eve.
As people huddled and cuddled, like you wouldn't believe.

Winter was here, they were thankful for snow.
But who should they thank? They just didn't know.

A talented artist had played Santa's elf.
By embracing the magic, she had found in herself.

So, the lesson my friends, should you feel you're adrift,
Is to just look within and find your true gift.

Embrace it and share it,
You're sure to shine bright.

Happy New Year to All
And to all a good night!

The End

Acknowledgements

I would like to take this opportunity to thank everyone who has helped with this book. First, I would like to thank Amy Minter for producing the movie, Kenney Myers and Tommy Zamberlan as associate producers and Benjamin Bryan as supervising producer of this holiday film. It feels like a long time coming, but without all of you, the movie or the book would never have come to be. I greatly appreciate every one of you and truly enjoy working with you!

I want to thank my good friend, Candy Cain for asking me to collaborate with her once again on this Christmas movie (and book) project. I'm thrilled to see the final product after the bumps and bruises along the way. As always, I really enjoyed working with you! Thanks again for asking me to be a part of this wonderful adventure.

Thank you to all of those that let us invade your space during filming. Especially our dear friend and colleague on-set, Michelle Perry, owner of Jon Michelle Hair Salon. You are always there to help, encourage and support and it's immensely appreciated!

I would like to thank Taryn Hacker and Cody Calafiore for bringing Noelle and Tyler to life in the film and on the pages. Thank you to Carrie Genzel, Patrick Muldoon, Sage Kermes, Andrew Fama, Yan-Kay Crystal Lowe, Frank Whaley, Terri Garber, Al Sapienza, Jennifer Bassey, James McBride and the rest of the incredibly talented cast who helped bring key characters to life. I truly enjoy watching all of you work! I loved working with everyone in the cast and crew. I've said it before, but so many of you have become like a family to me and I appreciate every single one of you! Being able to watch the story come together on screen is something incredibly difficult to describe and for a writer, that's not easy to admit. I'm thrilled to be able to tell stories in all these different ways and watch them come to life.

Thank you to Heartly Creations for designing the beautiful paperback and digital book covers and Benjamin Bryant, again, this time for the cover photo. Thank you again to Candy Cain and Gemelli Films for bringing this story to life. It turned out wonderful.

Thank you to Kelley and Nancy for all that you do and to all my Beta Readers and fans for your continued support. I greatly appreciate all your input and reviews. I value every one of you. Thank you, most of all, to my friends and family for their constant support and encouragement. I wouldn't be here without ALL of you. I love you all! No matter what time of year it is when you read this, Merry Christmas!

Connect with the Author

For more Family Contemporary Romance,
Read more by Nicole Mullaney or Ethan Dulane.
Connect with Nicole here:

Follow Me on Instagram
@nicolemullaney

Author Facebook Page
www.facebook.com/Nicole-Mullaney-Author-103006415283835/

BookBub
@NicoleMullaneyAuthor

For Adult Contemporary Romance,
Read books by Nikki A Lamers. Connect with her here:

Official Website
www.NikkiALamersauthor.com

https://linktr.ee/NikkiALamersauthor

For more information on Gemelli Films, find them here:

Official Website
http://Gemellifilm.com/

Gemelli Films Facebook Page
https://m.facebook.com/GemelliFilms/

About the Author

Nicole Mullaney has always had a passion for reading and writing, especially romance. She grew up in Wisconsin with her sister and mom and dad. She always loved reading romance books and watching romance movies with her dad, something they both enjoyed. She now lives on Long Island in New York with her husband and two kids. She spends her free time reading or hanging out with friends and family.

She met Candy Cain through her daughter Allison's acting career. A few years later, at the end of 2018, she began collaborating with her on these film/book projects; Ivy & Mistletoe their first project together in this capacity. She enjoys being able to watch the stories come to life in different ways and be a part of it from the beginning.